KV-512-290

2019
FEB 2020

2022

2024

2023

2024
2024

Port Talbot   McGregor. Rafe
es
lloedd   Six Strange Cases
l-nedd   2000670478
albot

ould be returned or renewed by the last date
above.
chwelyd llyfrau neu en hadnewyddu erbyn y
d olaf a nodir uchod.

Neath Library
Victoria Gardens
Neath
Tel: 01639 644604   LIB0044

2000670478

NEATH PORT TALBOT LIBRARIES

SPECIAL MESSAGE TO READERS

This book is published under the auspices of

THE ULVERSCROFT FOUNDATION

(registered charity No. 264873 UK)

Established in 1972 to provide funds for research, diagnosis and treatment of eye diseases. Examples of contributions made are: —

A Children's Assessment Unit at Moorfield's Hospital, London.

•

Twin operating theatres at the Western Ophthalmic Hospital, London.

•

A Chair of Ophthalmology at the Royal Australian College of Ophthalmologists.

•

The Ulverscroft Children's Eye Unit at the Great Ormond Street Hospital For Sick Children, London.

You can help further the work of the Foundation by making a donation or leaving a legacy. Every contribution, no matter how small, is received with gratitude. Please write for details to:

**THE ULVERSCROFT FOUNDATION,
The Green, Bradgate Road, Anstey,
Leicester LE7 7FU, England.
Telephone: (0116) 236 4325**

In Australia write to:
**THE ULVERSCROFT FOUNDATION,
c/o The Royal Australian and New Zealand
College of Ophthalmologists,
94-98 Chalmers Street, Surry Hills,
N.S.W. 2010, Australia**

SIX STRANGE CASES

Private investigator Titus Farrow is doomed by an encounter with the Chambers Scroll; Roderick Langham solves the mystery of the 'Demeter' from his armchair by the sea; a failed author goes in search of the barghest for inspiration; a missing person case turns even nastier than blackmail; Sweeney Todd meets his match . . . These stories make a gripping journey through 'The King in Yellow', 'Dracula', 'Sweeney Todd', and the noir fiction of the pulp era.

RAFE MCGREGOR

◆

SIX
STRANGE
CASES

Complete and Unabridged

LINFORD
Leicester

First published in Great Britain

First Linford Edition
published 2011

Copyright © 2010 by Rafe McGregor
All rights reserved

British Library CIP Data

McGregor, Rafe.
    Six strange cases. - -
(Linford mystery library)
1. Detective and mystery stories, English.
2. Large type books.
I. Title II. Series
823.9'2–dc22

ISBN 978–1–44480–572–7

Published by
F. A. Thorpe (Publishing)
Anstey, Leicestershire

Set by Words & Graphics Ltd.
Anstey, Leicestershire
Printed and bound in Great Britain by
T. J. International Ltd., Padstow, Cornwall

This book is printed on acid-free paper

NEATH PORT TALBOT
LIBRARIES

CL	
DATE	PP
LOC	NEA
NO	70478

To Gaylyn:
With love and regret.

Contents

The Short Spoon

Nobody likes coppers gone bad. We don't even like ourselves. Maybe that's why I'd do anything for Dicky Drake, or maybe it's because the Legion taught me the value of loyalty. I don't suppose the reason really matters.

Dicky, formerly Senior Officer Drake of Her Majesty's Prison Woodhill, and now landlord of the Globe Inn, was staring out the door. It was after closing time on Thursday night and Kobus, the barman, was cleaning up while I sipped on my Shiraz.

'Something there?' I asked.

He turned to me. He was in his early sixties, fit and slim except for a small belly, with a full head of hair and a silver goatee. 'Gurr's back. He's under the bridge.'

'Gurr?'

'That scrote I told you about. I barred him two months ago, but he's been back a

1

few times, threatening me. I think I'd better call the police again.'

'What's he doing?'

'Nothing at the moment.'

'Then they won't do anything. Let me go and have a word with him.'

'Are you sure? You've only been out a week.'

'It's alright. I'll be nice.'

I rose from the leather couch and joined Dicky. The Globe is on the bank of the Grand Union Canal, just north of Leighton Buzzard and Linslade, two small Bedfordshire towns that merged over the years. Globe Lane leads down from the Stoke Road and crosses the canal via an arched stone bridge a few dozen metres from the inn. Between the lights from the pub and the quarter moon, I could make out a man on the canalside, leaning against the abutment, hands in his pockets.

'Be careful,' said Dicky.

I gave him the look and walked out. At the risk of being immodest, although I'm only five foot eight, I weight two hundred and fifteen pounds, and — courtesy of having a lot of time to kill in prison — not much of it is fat. While I'm on about myself, I'm forty and ever since I was thrown down a cement staircase by a big Italian kid at school, I've either boxed or practiced aikido, and had regrettably numerous chances to exercise my skills. I gave the *Constance* — my forty-eight foot narrowboat — a quick glance, and passed a couple of other boats moored between the inn and the bridge.

Gurr was a tall, skinny chav, with a thick brown beard. He wore a dark tracksuit and Nike trainers, but had forgotten to put his hoodie up. He pushed off from the abutment as I approached, keeping his hands in his pockets. I stopped a couple of metres from him, careful to keep out of his personal space, and turned my body a fraction to the right. Up close, I noticed he had bad teeth and a tattoo of a pentagram on his left cheek. He grinned and I wondered if he was the full ticket.

'Evening,' I said. 'I think you'd better take yourself off before Mr Drake calls the coppers. Okay?'

He grinned again and produced a butterfly knife from his right pocket. He rotated his wrist outwards, flipping the handles open.

I pulled back my right fist, shuffled forward, and hit him straight in the mouth. I heard the snap of his two front teeth, felt the skin on one of my knuckles split.

Gurr dropped the knife and swayed back. He leant forward to try and regain his balance — I grabbed his anorak and pitched him into the canal. He disappeared under the water, then emerged, shouting and splashing. I picked up the butterfly knife, closed it, and dropped it in my pocket. I was about to head back to the Globe when I noticed how frantic and ineffectual his movements were.

'Can't swim!' he cried before swallowing a mouthful of Grand Union.

'You should have thought about that before you decided to play the hard man on the canalside, shouldn't you?'

Fortunately, Dicky had installed a life ring for just these circumstances. Or maybe they were for the kids that fell in when they were feeding the swans. I tossed Gurr the ring and he held on as if his life depended on it — which I suppose it did.

'Kick your fucking legs.'

Eventually, he propelled himself to the edge. I grabbed him by the hair and assisted his return to *terra firma*. He fell heavily — no cat, this muppet — and started scrabbling to his feet.

I pulled his head back, smacked his left ear with the flat of my hand, and shoved him towards the path.

He spat at me — missed — and broke into a run. Up the path, across the bridge, and away into the trees.

I picked up the life ring, put it back, and turned to see Dicky surrounded by three large men.

Royston Swingewood was in his late forties. A broad, stocky six-one; shaved head, callused knuckles. For a former boxer his nose and ears were remarkably unblemished, though he had a long scar across the back of his skull. He was wearing a dark blue suit, white shirt without a tie, and Italian leather shoes.

Galliano and Malloy were also Londoners, despite their names. Galliano was as big as his boss, in his early thirties, and always had a five o'clock shadow on the go. Malloy was a few years younger, and even bigger — but fat with it — his blonde hair perpetually slicked back with Brylcreem. It was one of the few times I'd seen him without his sunglasses.

Swingewood lifted his hands and clapped three times.

Before spending five years and three months in Woodhill for manslaughter, I'd been a beat copper in Islington. I'd arrested Galliano and Malloy twice each, but hadn't been able to put them away. I had closed down one of Swingewood's most lucrative chop shops, however, so I was surprised when he'd put the word out that I wasn't to be touched. Dicky arranging me the job as a Segregation Unit cleaner was what really saved my hide, but Swingewood thought I owed him, and I knew he'd come to collect.

'I'm glad you haven't gone soft. I hear it's like Butlins inside these days.'

Dicky didn't know who they were, but

he knew it wasn't a social call. I noticed Galliano was wearing gloves and carrying a black briefcase. 'What can I do for you, Swingewood?'

Malloy surged forward, but Swingewood grabbed his arm. 'Easy, son, Farrow's always been a cheeky twat. I heard you'd become a water pikey, so this old geezer's gonna to have to stay open for another half hour.'

I shrugged and said, 'I'm sorry, Dicky.'

He nodded and went back in. I followed him, and got a noseful of oranges as I passed Galliano. He always doused himself in Miller Harris Citron eau de cologne, which I reckoned pretty camp for an enforcer.

When we were all inside, Swingewood said: 'Four shots of your finest single malt, no ice or water. Then you can piss off.'

Kobus started to reply, but Dicky sent him packing. I resumed my seat on the couch and the three of them sat opposite me, a low table between us. No one spoke as Dicky brought the drinks over on a tray, and locked the front door. 'Are you sure?' he asked me.

'It's fine.'

'I'll be upstairs.'

Swingewood started as soon as Dicky was out of sight. 'Tomorrow afternoon you have a meeting with a dodgy book dealer in Belgravia. I know you're supposed to be a clever cock as well, but I've got a checklist for you. I want you to — '

'Just a minute. You want me to go and buy you a book?'

Swingewood sighed. 'You're in my pocket. That means you don't ask questions, you do as you told. If I wanted you to buy me a book, you'd ask me *which one, Mr Swingewood.* Or, you could give me lip and I could have this place — and the old geezer — burnt to the ground. You're not a copper anymore, Farrow. You're on the outside, the *other* side, and that's *my* side. You work for me for as long as I say so. If you're lucky, it won't be for the full five years you owe me. Now, *may* I continue this conversation, or are you going to interrupt again?'

'No, Mr Swingewood.'

'That's better. Don't you know the economy's gone to ratshit? I thought you all had tellies inside now? There's a lot of money in old books, and they don't go bust like banks. A pukka first edition Shakespeare goes for around two and a half million quid, if and when you can find one. This Graham knob has two books I'm interested in and the original manuscript of something called *The King in Yellow* — '

'By Robert Chambers. I read it in the nick.'

'I don't give a fuck. I want you to check out the three books tomorrow afternoon, then go back tomorrow night and rip him off. He'll be up to his eyeballs in security, so you're just going to have to go across the pavement and stick a gun in his face. Once you've confirmed the goods, Acutt will ring him up to make sure he's there — alone — in the evening.'

Swingewood turned to Galliano, and he put the briefcase on the table, nudging two of the glasses out the way. I downed the last of my wine and picked up the whisky.

'There's a shooter in there, and a mobile. Keep them when you're done. Bring me the books in the case at Filthy McNasty's tomorrow at midnight. Acutt and Tennant will be waiting for you. The combination is zero, one, one, eight.' Swingewood smiled.

One, one, eight was my old PC number, and Acutt and Tennant were Swingewood's top dogs. 'I'm not going to kill anyone.'

'I'm not expecting you to. Put the shooter in his face, he'll wet himself. Get him to open the safe — or whatever — just get the fucking books.'

'He's going to know it's me.'

'Not my problem. He thinks your name is Trotman. Wear a mask or something. Make sure you don't get nicked. If you do, you're on your own this time.'

Trotman was the name of the man I'd killed. The jokes were all on me tonight.

Galliano turned the briefcase around and I opened it. Inside, there was a silver Taurus .38 Special with a two inch barrel and a black rubber grip; a ludicrously small mobile phone; a box of fifty .38

10

Special rounds; and a couple of typed sheets of A4.

'Acutt will phone you at midday to check you haven't bottled it. Make sure you don't. Phone him back when you've seen the books. If you bring him the swag on time, he'll throw in a couple of tons for your trouble, and I'll consider part of your debt settled. It's always useful for me to have an ex-copper on the payroll and you won't find many other career opportunities coming your way.'

I had no choice. All of my colleagues had abandoned me when I went down, and Dicky was my only friend on the right side of the law. Actually, he was my only friend, end-of. I didn't have protection from anyone, and I didn't feel like getting the shit kicked out of me if I could avoid it. More importantly, if I didn't do exactly what I was told, Dicky would suffer. Like I said, I had no choice. I nodded slowly.

'Then, we'll drink to it.' He raised his glass and his goons followed suit.

I picked up my own and swigged it back in one gulp.

Swingewood smacked his lips and rose — we all followed suit. He stepped out the way to allow Malloy past, and put his hand on my arm to steer me towards the bar. I thought it was strange, but I guessed he was trying to assert his dominance. 'Don't fuck this up, Farrow.'

'I won't, but I'd appreciate it if you don't send those two back here.'

'I won't have to, will I?' He smiled again and followed his men out. I locked the door behind them and picked up the briefcase. There were only four glasses on the table: my wine glass and three tumblers. I wondered which one of them was the kleptomaniac.

*   *   *

I turned off Sloane Street and walked into Eaton Square, which isn't a square at all. It's an elongated oblong arranged around a shitload of private gardens; a leafy, luxurious enclave of stucco-fronted classical terraces between the street of the same name and King's Road. Graham's five-storey house doubled as his business premises, and was on the south side of the non-square. I was dressed in suit, tie, and a pair of Henley lace-ups, smoking a Gauloise Blonde. It was the only legacy of my time in France other than a taste for cheap red wine. I fired the fag into the gutter and pressed Graham's buzzer at exactly five minutes past one.

A few moments later the solid oak door was answered by the man himself. Graham was about thirty, six-two, fat, and pompous. He had ruddy cheeks that probably made him look younger than he really was, and short black hair with a long fringe he probably thought looked cool. He was wearing a tailored green suit, silk shirt, and chunky tie. He regarded me with disdain and didn't offer his hand. 'Mr Trotman?'

'Yeah.'

'I'm Douggie Graham. Come in.' His accent was beyond public school — it bordered on Royal Family. 'Know much about books, do you?'

I stepped inside and he closed the door behind me. 'I know more about money.'

'Quite so.' He waddled off, leading me

past a door on the left, and up a richly-carpeted staircase.

When we reached the first floor, he opened a set of double doors into a magnificent reception room, with a chandelier, fireplace, floor-to-ceiling windows overlooking the square, and two large sash windows overlooking a garden. The minimalist design focused attention on two long, cream sofas arranged around a glass coffee table. My attention was focused on the one nearest the gilt-edged mirror, on the magnificent example of the female of the species perched thereon. She had honey-blonde shoulder-length hair, an English Rose complexion, and full lips painted dark salmon. Except for her wide mouth, her features were exquisitely refined, and accentuated by stylish retro glasses. She was shapely in a similarly refined way, dressed in a fawn cord blazer and long, buff skirt.

'Mr Trotman, this is Ms Beggs. If you'll wait a minute or two, I'll prepare the manuscripts for examination.'

I smiled as I sat on the other sofa. 'Hello, Ms Beggs, nice to meet you.'

'Charlotte, please.'

She returned my smile, and I immediately started thinking how good she'd look naked. It wasn't so much that I'd been in prison for five years — she just oozed sex appeal.

'Are you also a buyer?' I asked.

'Yes.' She smiled again, and brushed a nonexistent strand of hair from her face. 'This is one of Douggie's many bad habits, I'm afraid. He never arranges private viewings. He likes to have two or three people present to play them off against each other. I wonder. If you don't mind me saying, you don't look like a book collector.'

'Only if you don't mind me saying that you're far too foxy to be a book dealer.' She tried to hide her blush, but failed. 'And I'm not. I'm here for someone else.'

'So am I. Maybe Douggie's strategy will work against him today.'

Unfortunately, Graham returned before I could find out any more about Charlotte. 'Thank you for your patience. Please follow me.'

Charlotte picked up her attaché case and we went out to the landing. I estimated that the reception room took up most of the first floor. I held out my arm for Charlotte to proceed, but she responded in kind. A shame. I'd been hoping to examine her rear, now she'd have to put up with mine in her face.

On the second floor we were ushered into another big room, with more furniture and more of a businesslike feel to it. I noted a small balcony on the other side of a French door. There were dreary portraits on the walls, a leather chaise longue, two antique chairs, and a mahogany console. The top of the console was fitted with a baize cloth — not unlike a pool table — and there were three books on top of that. To the right of the last were half a dozen pairs of white gloves.

The nearest book was A4-sized, and bound in a leather cover without any indication of title or author. The middle one was about seven by five inches, bound in red cloth with gold lettering that read: 'The Hound of the Baskervilles' at the top and 'Conan Doyle' at the bottom. There was a picture of a black dog under the title. The third book was of a similar size, with yellow cloth and orange lettering that read: 'Dracula By Bram Stoker'.

'Before you have a closer look at the selection, may I ask you to please wear a pair of the gloves before touching them? Thank you. *The Hound of the Baskervilles* is of course the most popular of all the Sherlock Holmes stories. That is a first edition, published by George Newnes and Company of *The Strand* fame in 1902. The *Dracula* is also a first, by Archibald Constable and Company in 1897. In addition, it is a presentation copy signed by the author. Lastly, the Chambers Scroll. The original manuscript of the unpublished play by Robert W. Chambers, entitled *The King in Yellow*, to which he alluded in his 1895 anthology of short stories, published under the same title. It is written in his hand, inscribed as being completed in Paris in 1889, and has been calf-bound with a sewn spine. Help yourselves.'

Charlotte removed a pair of gloves from her case. I took a memo pad from my jacket pocket, skipped past the list of tools I'd need when I came back tonight, and peered at the *Dracula*. Graham was hovering, obviously concerned I was going to ignore his instructions regarding the gloves. Charlotte picked up the Chambers Scroll very gently, as if she were lifting a newborn baby.

'You can open that up for me,' I said to Graham, 'so I can check it isn't falling to bits.'

'I assure you it is not.' Graham donned a pair of the gloves. 'You can see both the first editions are in excellent condition considering they are over a hundred years old.' He opened the book without lifting it from the console, and turned several of the pages carefully. 'Satisfied?'

'No chance.' I checked the next point on my pad. 'I want to see that it doesn't have a *Shoulder of Shasta* advertisement, whatever that is.' Graham was taken aback, which made me want to play the boor even more, but I didn't want Charlotte thinking I was a fool.

'It doesn't. This is the first edition, first state, as I'm sure Ms Beggs will confirm. This is where the advertisement would be were it a second state publication.' He opened the book to the rear, showing a blank page.

Charlotte appeared not to have heard her name.

'Alright. Same again with *The Hound of the Baskervilles*.' Graham repeated his performance. 'This one's also got something that shouldn't be there. *Published 1902* not printed on the copyright page. Let me see.'

'There,' he said, 'that's the copyright page. There's no date.'

He was right. Meanwhile, Charlotte had replaced the Chambers Scroll on the console and was examining one of the pages in detail. I put my pad away. 'I'm not interested in the Scroll unless you want to make it worth my while, but I'll take both of these.'

Graham's mouth dropped open, reminding me of a goldfish. 'I say, you've hardly looked at them and we — '

'How much for the two together. Cash.'

'Er, I think we'd better wait until Ms Beggs has had a look.'

Charlotte waved one of her gloved hands without looking up. 'I'm not interested in the firsts, Douggie, just the Chambers manuscript.'

'And I'm not interested in Chambers, so let's get on with it.'

'Er, yes, perhaps you'd rather discuss this in private?'

Remembering my brief conversation with Charlotte, I replied: 'That was the original plan, but seeing as Charlotte's here, I don't want to be rude. Name your price.'

'I suppose, for a cash buy for both, I could offer you a small discount and put the total price at a hundred and sixty thousand pounds.'

'Call it a hundred and fifty,' I said.

Graham acted as if he was considering the offer and Charlotte looked at me and winked. 'You're not a collector are you, Mr Trotman?'

'No, I'm not.'

'I'd ask for the prices separately first,' she said.

Graham glared at her, and she smiled, revealing slightly crooked white teeth.

'My minimum price for both books is eighty-five thousand pounds each.'

Charlotte picked up *The Hound of the Baskervilles*. She paged through it quickly, and Graham winced. Then she replaced it and said, 'That's about right for *The Hound*; the *Dracula* isn't worth more than fifty thousand at the absolute limit.'

I cut him off before he could say anything: 'Eighty-five plus fifty equals one thirty-five. Call it one twenty-five with my discount.'

'I'm not sure if I can go that low . . . '

'Unless you want to throw in the Scroll as well?'

'Hardly. You'll agree the Scroll is as genuine as the other two, Charlotte?'

'Yes, it seems so. I have handwriting samples copied from his letters at the University of Virginia. I'm not a qualified graphologist, but the match is enough to satisfy me, and the paper matches other manuscripts of his. Chambers was in Paris in 1889, and although he was a painter, he'd already completed his first novel, which he published anonymously.

There's a note on the first page that reads *not for publication under any circumstances*, followed by an exclamation mark, which might be why he never submitted it for publication. But you know what I'm going to ask, don't you?'

'I do, and you know my answer.'

'We're talking about a unique manuscript, Douggie. There's no standard against which the Chambers Scroll can be verified, which means that provenance *is* an issue.'

Graham smiled smugly, and raised his chubby palms. 'Why don't we say that the lack of provenance offsets the uniqueness and take it from there? Need I remind you that thirteen pages of the manuscript of Conan Doyle's *Last Bow* are coming up for auction next month. They're expected to fetch at least a hundred and fifty thousand pounds.'

'A hundred thousand, actually, but point taken. On the other hand, you must accept the problem regarding the provenance.'

Graham grinned. 'A compromise, I agree.'

'How much do you want for the Chambers Scroll?'

'Oh, no, my dear Charlotte. Ladies first. How much are you prepared to offer?'

'A hundred and fifty thousand pounds, unless you tell me where it came from.'

I winked at Charlotte. 'I'll give you a quarter million for the lot.'

'Excuse me, Mr Trotman, but I thought you weren't interested in the Scroll.'

'My boss doesn't like people taking the piss, and neither do I. His offer is two fifty for the three, or one twenty-five for the two. He might call you back; he might not. I'll let myself out. Charlotte, it was absolutely a pleasure.'

She inclined her head and smiled back. 'Such a gentleman. I do hope we meet again.'

I trotted back down the stairs, left the building, and phoned Acutt. I told him there was definitely a hundred and thirty-five grand's worth of rare books in the place, and possibly double that. Then I went shopping for battle.

★　★　★

I returned to Eaton Square at ten past nine that evening. I was wearing a completely new set of clothes so as to minimise any potential for DNA: a grey baseball cap pulled low, and a navy blue mackintosh with the collar turned up, over a dark Jasper Conran suit. It was raining lightly; ideal because the drizzle explained my get-up on such a mild evening. My raised collar also hid a balaclava, worn around my neck and stretched so that I could pull it up from the bottom as opposed to down from the top — no room to hide it under the cap. I had a pair of thin leather gloves on, worn over a pair of surgical gloves, and Swingewood's briefcase. I wasn't unrecognisable, but the change would probably be enough to keep my identity within reasonable doubt when London's notorious camera coverage was examined for evidence.

As for Graham himself, he'd only met me briefly and I had one more card to play. It was hardly an ace up my sleeve, but it might do the trick. I'm no loss to the stage, but I can put on a relatively convincing French accent, and I can also speak French fluently with a slight English accent. A posh bloke like Graham would have at least a smattering of French and even if he didn't understand entirely, the gun in his face would help get the message across. They tend to do that, guns, break down barriers between people.

I saw Graham's place ahead and noted the balcony on the second floor. It was too far up to be useful as an escape route. There'd be a rear entrance on the ground floor if everything went pear-shaped. It might only lead to an enclosed garden, but there would have to be an alley somewhere — even the rich have to get rid of their rubbish. I hunched my neck into my shoulders for the benefit of the public and privately-owned CCTV and pressed the buzzer.

The ball was in play.

I was deliberately late, in order to unsettle Graham and ensure he was poised to answer the door.

I counted out five seconds, the tempo of my heart faster with each one, then slipped off the leather gloves and put them in the left hand pocket of my mac. I reached into my collar and dragged up the balaclava. I lifted the baseball cap and pulled the mask over my forehead, so that it covered all of my face except for the bridge of my nose and my eyes. Then I fitted the cap back on my head, hunched lower into my mac, and picked up the briefcase in my left hand.

I heard the door being unlocked; Graham opened it. He did the goldfish thing at the same time as my right fist folded his nose into his face. He staggered back, clutching at the damage. I stepped in, dropped the briefcase, and shut the door. Give him his due: he bellowed and charged towards me.

A big, heavy bloke, but not a fighter. I moved left and shot my left fist into his temple. It knocked him off balance and I kicked his legs from under him; the fall expelled the wind from his lungs. I bent down, rolled him over, and sat on his back. He had a little bit of fight left, but it ended when I showed him the revolver.

In French, I said, 'Do exactly what I say, Mr Graham, starting with keeping very still. Do you understand?'

He replied in French accented much better than mine that he did. There's nothing to beat a public school education.

'Are we alone? I warn you, if you lie now, I will shoot anyone that surprises me first, and then ask you who they were.'

'We're alone.'

'No servants, family, girlfriend, boyfriend, bodyguard?'

'No.'

'Keep still.'

I climbed off his back and removed the baseball cap, which made me look an idiot if nothing else. I stuffed it in my pocket, picked up the briefcase, and made sure the front door was locked. Graham didn't move, not even to stop his nose from bleeding all over his embroidered carpet. I kept two arm's lengths away from him and told him to stand up and take his jacket off. He saw the claret and collapsed. I thought he was going to pass out.

'Mr Graham!'

He held his nose and moaned while I dropped the briefcase and rifled his jacket pockets for a hanky. I tossed it over to him — monogrammed, of course — and grabbed the case.

'Get up and take me to the books. If you try anything I'll shoot you in the leg first, then the knee, then a bit higher. Do you understand? Good. Off you go.'

I kept four or five steps behind Graham, who leant heavily on the banister with his left hand while pressing the hanky to his nose with his right. We went past the first floor reception to the second floor viewing room and then up again to the third floor. There was only one above us, which had to be the master bedroom.

The third floor landing was small, with three doors leading off from it. Graham turned left, as if to continue up the stairs, but opened the door on the Eaton Square side of the house. The room was of average size, with sash windows, floor-to-ceiling book shelves, and two built-in cupboards. There were also two leather easy chairs, each with a footrest, and a side table in-between.

'What do you want?' asked Graham through his hanky.

'The Chambers Scroll and . . . ' I pretended to consider the size of the briefcase ' . . . Your two most valuable books.'

He groaned. 'I'll be ruined.'

'You're not insured?' He groaned again. 'Get a move on or it'll be your life insurance that's the problem.'

Graham fumbled in his trouser pocket and produced a set of keys, which he used to open the larger of the cupboards. There was a safe inside, about half my height, and bolted to the wall.

'When you unlock it, I want you to step back without opening it. Do you understand?'

He nodded.

If it was mine, I'd have kept a weapon inside for a last-ditch defence of my property.

Graham entered a long series of numbers onto an electronic keypad and I heard a whirr and a click. He stepped away and I gestured for him to sit in one of the chairs and put his feet up. Once they were off the ground I opened the safe with my free hand. There were three compartments; two contained books, the other stacked envelopes and sheets of paper. There were about a dozen volumes in total, including the calfskin manuscript of the Chambers Scroll. I jerked my head at Graham and he returned to the safe, taking even more care not to bleed on any of the books. He withdrew the Chambers Scroll first, then two slim volumes: *A Select Collection of Original Scottish Airs* by Burns, and *Tamerlane*, by Poe. He stacked all three on the deep-pile carpet next to him, and looked up at me.

'There you are.'

I punched him in the right temple again.

He screamed, bounced off the cupboard door, and curled up in a ball on the floor.

I checked he wasn't faking, then knelt in front of the safe myself. *The Hound of the Baskervilles* and *Dracula* were easy to find. I removed them, glanced over at

Graham again, and put the revolver in my pocket. I opened my briefcase, took out three coiled ropes, placed the three books inside, and locked it.

'There's only thirty copies of *Tamerlane*,' Graham mumbled from behind the cover of his forearms, 'and the Burns is signed.'

'Get up, we're done here. Do exactly as I say and you won't be hurt anymore. And pick up your hanky — you're bleeding again. You can lock the safe up if you want.'

He did want. He returned the two volumes, and locked both the safe and the cupboard — all with one hand.

'Back downstairs.' Holding the brief-case in my left hand and the ropes in my right I followed him to the second floor.

'Stop. Open that door, the one straight ahead. Put the lights on as you go.' I'd intended to tie him to one of the antique chairs, but I wasn't sure how strong they were. There was a door to the left. 'Open that one. Inside.' The room was small and sparsely furnished, but there was a dark, hardwood table, and a solitary chair, which wasn't overstuffed. Perfect. 'Put the keys on the table and sit there.'

Graham obeyed, placing his elbows on the table and leaning forward, the crimson hanky still pressed to his nostrils.

There was a single sash window overlooking the garden to the rear. I set the briefcase down, closed the curtains, and scooped up Graham's keys. 'There are two ways we can do this,' I said as I flexed the first rope. 'You can either be conscious or unconscious. Unconscious is easier for me, but I recommend conscious for you, so carry on doing what I tell you. Also, I'm not going to gag you. With all that blood up your nose you could suffocate. If you fuck me around, I'll change my mind. Are we clear?'

He nodded.

'Good. Kneel down in front of the table and put your hands behind your back.'

I tied his hands up securely and then sat him back in the chair. I used the other ropes to tie his elbows and ankles to the wood. He bitched for a bit, but didn't struggle. The gagging was just a threat. I wouldn't risk killing him, and I reckoned the house was soundproofed anyway.

When I was satisfied Graham wasn't going anywhere in the next few hours, I picked up the briefcase and switched off the light.

'You can't leave me here!' he shouted in English. 'They won't find me for days. I'll die — don't leave me!'

'Shut up! In a couple of hours I'm going to call the police. Sit tight and don't panic.'

I closed the door and put the keys in the lock, but didn't fasten it. I trotted down the stairs to the entrance hall. Everything had gone to plan — so far — but I wanted to wash my face and take a few minutes before the next stage of the job. I guessed the kitchen would be on the ground floor and it was, first door on the left. The room was huge, with porcelain floor tiles, pine cupboards, granite worktops, and lots of stainless steel. There was a small breakfast room to the right, and stairs to the lower ground floor on the left. I made for the sink and caught a faint whiff of oranges.

Probably from the fruit bowl in the breakfast room.

I turned on the cold tap, removed the

balaclava, and splashed my face with water. I was careful to roll the balaclava into a ball so as not to leave my DNA all over the shop. I put the baseball cap back on and stuffed the balaclava in my pocket. A couple of gulps of water, then I turned the tap off. I removed the surgical gloves, fitted them into each other, and put them in my pocket as well. I put the leather gloves on and took a few deep breaths.

I picked up the briefcase and returned to the front door, ready to depart. I set the latch on the door so that it wouldn't lock when I closed it — ready for the arrival of the cavalry after I made my anonymous call. I checked my collar was high, and my cap low. Then I took a few more breaths to calm myself. As casually as possible, I stepped out into the night and shut the door behind me. So far so good. I turned right, destination Victoria Tube, but didn't hurry.

I managed about thirty paces.

Oranges, fucking oranges.

There hadn't been any oranges in the fruit bowl, only bananas and apples.

'Fuck, fuck, fuck,' I said aloud as I turned around and walked back.

Rough Graham up and steal his books — I could live with that. Be responsible for his death — no way.

I never seem to learn.

★ ★ ★

I stopped outside the door and pretended to press the buzzer. Then I pretended to do it again, buying some time. After nearly a minute outside Graham's door I opened it quickly and quietly, and darted inside.

I could smell oranges in the hall.

I locked the front door, took out the Taurus, and stashed the briefcase under the stairs. From here, I could see the back door, which was something of a relief. Then, without knowing why the hell I was doing it, I crept upstairs. I reached the first floor and kept going, following my nose.

There was a light coming from the second floor — I'd definitely switched them off.

My heart was beating so hard and fast I thought everyone would hear me.

One of the reasons I don't like a snub-nosed .38 is that it's too small to hold with two hands. Ideally, a handgun should be fired with both hands around the grip, exerting pressure from either side, and keeping the weapon steady. Two hands also gives stability against recoil for the next shot. If you're firing with one hand, the best stance is side on, gun arm extended to shoulder height, like they used to teach coppers years ago. Not likely to achieve the best results, although it does make the shooter more difficult to hit if fire is returned.

I broke out into a sweat at the thought.

I reached the room where Graham had shown us his wares — the door was open, lights on — so was the room where I'd left him.

I heard Graham's voice: 'What are you doing. No! No!'

I entered the first room, saw three people in the second.

Time stood still.

Graham was sitting in the chair,

struggling against his bonds. Galliano was standing a couple of metres away from him, on the right, and Malloy on the left. They both had pistols in their right hands. Malloy had what looked like a freezer bag in his left.

Galliano raised his nine-mil.

Graham bellowed.

I raised the Taurus, aiming for Galliano's head.

The two handguns fired simultaneously — Graham's head snapped back, Galliano fell.

Malloy spun around — shock on his face.

He was less than three metres away, and he hadn't lifted his weapon yet.

Unlucky.

I pumped two rounds into his chest. He dropped the bag and his pistol came up as he went down. I shot him in the head, just to make sure. He fell backwards, dropping his weapon.

I dashed over to Galliano. He was still clutching his gun, one of the Glock 17 variants. I put my right foot on his forearm, and kicked the Glock away with my left.

Galliano was bleeding profusely and keening unintelligibly. So was Malloy, on the other side of the room. Graham was the only one silent. His lips twitched for a few seconds as I watched, but his head had already sagged back and his eyes were gone. He was bleeding from a small red hole in the middle of his forehead and a larger exit wound behind his right ear.

Poor bastard.

I glanced back at Galliano, who managed, 'Farrow — you!'

Yeah, me.

I noted Galliano was wearing surgical gloves. I had to keep out of the blood, which was either spattered or pooling over most of the room on Graham's side of the table. I stepped across Galliano and went back to Malloy. He was also wearing gloves, covered in his blood as he held his head.

I only had one live round left in the Taurus. I contemplated picking up Malloy's Browning, but I didn't want to complicate matters.

I couldn't reload with my leather gloves on, so I pulled the left glove off with my teeth and kept it in my mouth while I found a fistful of spare rounds in my pocket. I didn't have time to be careful, so I swung out the cylinder and depressed the extractor rod, ejecting all five cartridges. I loaded four live rounds, and knelt down to retrieve the one from the floor. Then I snapped the cylinder shut.

Once I'd reloaded, my heart rate started to slow. I put the glove back on and picked up the four empty casings from the floor. As I stood up with the last one in my hand, I noticed Malloy's package.

The plastic bag contained a glass. Or, more accurately, a tumbler, of the sort one might use to drink single malt whisky.

A wave of rage seized me — my body temperature rose. I growled and turned to Malloy, ready to kick the son of a bitch to death. Common-sense took over. He was on his last legs anyway. I vented my anger on the evidence instead, stamping on it about a dozen times, then crushing the shards.

Across the room, Galliano was also heading west.

Get the hell out.

I kept the Taurus in my hand, put both in my mac pocket. Forcing myself to draw slow, deep breaths, I walked back down the stairs, leaving the smell of gunpowder behind.

Keep calm, breath, slow it down.

Even if the neighbours had heard anything, they wouldn't think there'd been a massacre — not in Belgravia. They'd think it was a DVD, or Play-Station.

Keep calm, keep moving.

I'd stopped sweating by the time I reached the ground floor. I picked the briefcase up and considered the options. Galliano and Malloy had probably come in through the back door, so I should go out the front. It would take balls of steel, but I had to repeat exactly what I'd just done ten minutes or less ago.

I walked to the door, stopped, and let go of the revolver in my pocket. I took one last deep breath, checked my collar was up, and my cap down. No need to set the latch now, so I opened the door and —

Two men stared at me: a tall, broad Afro-Caribbean with dreadlocks and a goatee; a shorter, slimmer Caucasian with blonde hair and a dark tan. Bernie Tennant and Paul Acutt, both carrying.

'The briefcase!' Acutt pointed.

Tennant raised an enormous black pistol.

I slammed the door closed — relieved to hear the click of the latch — turned, and bolted for the rear entrance.

There was a boom like a cannon.

I looked back as I ducked under the stairs — the front door splintered. The gun was probably a .50 calibre Desert Eagle. Even a nick from one will blow a big chunk out of you.

I reached the back door and grabbed the handle, hoping Galliano and Malloy hadn't locked it. They hadn't. I charged out into a small, neat garden, with high hedges on either side. Galliano and Malloy must have entered via a covered alleyway. I could use the same one to make good my escape.

I stopped.

Left or right?

I heard a noise from behind, Acutt and Tennant on their way.

I was about to go left, when I changed my mind. One of my pursuers might be waiting in Eaton Square. I continued straight ahead, through a small grove of trees, and reached a high brick wall — too high to climb. I turned right, ran along the wall until I came to another hedge. It was a couple of feet taller than me, so I kept going, hurled the briefcase over, and leapt. I hit the hedge, and scrabbled with both hands and feet. My momentum was enough to take me over as the branches sagged beneath me. I landed heavily, rolled, and jumped to my feet.

I was in another private garden, with a neat green in the middle. There was a fountain on the green, but no service entrance in sight.

More noise from behind.

I picked up the briefcase and took a few steps forward, desperate to find a gap in the surrounding walls. A security light came on — I swore — broke into a jog. As I drew level with the fountain I noticed a raised patio up ahead on the left, barely visible in a forest of pot plants, yellow and purple vines, and more hedges. I bounded onto the terrace, saw a set of French doors under a balcony, and pumped my legs fast. I hugged the briefcase, angled my body to the left, ducked down, and threw myself at the doors.

They imploded in a mass of glass and wood.

I stumbled, rolled, and slid along a polished wooden floor. I heard a high-pitched scream. I crashed into a glass coffee table — which slid into a cream sofa — and saw a man and a woman jump up from the dining table behind.

Nothing like open-plan to prevent injuries.

The woman kept screaming, the man's mouth just hung open.

I clambered to my feet and drew the Taurus. 'Where's the front door? The front door!'

He pointed ahead of me and I ran to an entrance hall. I pocketed the revolver, opened the door, and burst out into Boscobel Place. I turned left into

Elizabeth Street, and left again into Chester Square. I eased my pace to a trot, glancing back every few seconds. I couldn't see any sign of pursuit, but I could hear sirens, definitely headed this way. I found a small park, took cover in the shadows of some trees, and rested.

My heart was beating a tattoo again, my breathing shallow, and I was sweating like a rapist. I took the Taurus from my mac and set it on the briefcase. Then I took the empty cartridges from the other pocket and switched them to my trousers. I removed my cap and mac, folded them up into a small bundle, and shoved it under a shrub. Not ideal, but there was no space in the briefcase. I stood back up, felt a wave of nausea, and swallowed down hard. I dusted myself off of leaves and glass, and wiped my face to check for any open wounds. There weren't any.

I placed the Taurus and my leather gloves in the briefcase and headed for Victoria Tube, choosing a roundabout route. I was taking a risk by walking rather than running, but I wanted to avoid drawing any attention to myself. I kept my pace casual, and kept calm when the sirens closed in and I heard the police helicopter overhead.

I reached Victoria seven minutes later without incident, but with a huge appetite. All the excitement had burned off my energy and my body demanded immediate replacement. I found a Burger King, ordered three Whoppers and the biggest Coke they served. I took my tray over to an unoccupied table, selected a seat facing the door, and fed.

Swingewood wanted me to go down for murdering Graham.

That explained why he was so interested in a relatively small investment. What he was really after was putting me back in prison. I had no idea I'd pissed him off so much when I was a copper. Or perhaps he was doing the job for someone else. It didn't matter, because nobody likes coppers gone bad. Galliano and Malloy must have already been in the house when I'd first arrived. I had no idea how they'd managed it, and that didn't matter either. Malloy's plan was to plant the glass, with my fingerprints on it.

I started getting angry all over again.

I tried to keep calm and think about what should be happening now. I was supposed to be on my way to Filthy McNasty's while Galliano and Malloy disappeared into the night after killing Graham and planting the tumbler. Swingewood would have tipped off the police and there'd be a firearms unit waiting for me at the pub. I'd stroll in with the late Douggie Graham's precious books in my briefcase; the only thing that wouldn't fit would be my Taurus.

I thought about it some more, and realised I had a long night ahead of me.

★   ★   ★

I felt someone come aboard the narrowboat.

Even though I knew there was a chance I'd miscalculated, and that the mistake might cost me my life, I kept my eyes closed and rolled onto my front.

'Armed Police — keep still!'

I heard footsteps — men running — saw light from a powerful flashlight

46

through my closed lids. I felt a man put his knee on my back and I didn't fight. He grabbed my wrists, handcuffed me.

Seconds later I was hauled up so that I was sitting on the edge of the bed, in my boxers. Someone switched on the light and I saw three Specialist Firearms Officers in full assault kit. One lowered the Heckler & Koch MP5 he'd been pointing at me; another holstered his Glock; the third, who'd cuffed me, stepped away and shouted: 'Clear!'

I was glad I hadn't locked the doors before I went to bed — they would've smashed them in. I heard someone else climb aboard, and a fourth man ducked his head under the door and descended the three stairs to the deck. He was tall and pale, slim but jowly, with discoloured teeth and greying blonde hair. He was wearing a suit, tie, and overcoat.

'Titus Farrow?' he asked.

'Just Farrow.'

'DI Moon, Met Homicide. I'm arresting you on suspicion of the murder of Louis Galliano and Kenneth Malloy. You do not have to say anything, but it may harm your defence if you do not mention when questioned something you later rely on in court. Anything you say may be given in evidence, but you already know all that, don't you?'

When Moon named Galliano and Malloy rather than all three of the dead men, I started shitting myself. How much did he know?

'DS Krishnan is going to search this boat for a firearm. You can either give me permission to conduct the search, or I'll wait for the warrant — I don't give a fuck.'

'Crack on. You won't find anything illegal. And make sure you lock up when you're done.' Moon glared at me. 'Can I get dressed now?'

'Take the cuffs off,' he said to the SFO. 'Stay where you are, the officers will fetch your gear.'

When I'd dressed, I was cuffed again — hands in front this time — and led from the *Constance*. It was ten to five and I was exhausted. Five other armed officers were standing in the dark, with three men in plainclothes. One of the latter was talking to Dicky in the doorway of the Globe. I smiled at him before being led off an unmarked car. I thought I'd be driven to London, but our destination was the local Leighton Buzzard station. I was processed by the custody sergeant and had to wait a few hours for a legal representative. The circus eventually began at ten, but that's all it was, a circus.

I was knackered because I'd spent the rest of Friday night and Saturday morning burying the briefcase — complete with Taurus, spare rounds, and mobile — in the trees, and cleaning myself, everything I'd been wearing, and every inch of the interior of the narrowboat. I'd even vacuumed.

The CCTV evidence was inconclusive and although I didn't have an alibi worth the name, I didn't need to prove my innocence; they needed to prove my guilt. We all knew I was going to walk. Moon gave up the ghost at half-five on Saturday evening and released me without charge.

On my way back to the Globe, I stopped at a call box and phoned Swingewood.

Five hours later I was sitting on my favourite leather couch, next to the bar of the Globe. Tennant, Swingewood, and Acutt sat opposite, the briefcase on the table between us. They were all dressed in smart suits, with surprisingly little bling. Dicky had retired upstairs at my request.

'I don't want any more trouble, Mr Swingewood. *The Hound of the Baskervilles* and the Chambers Scroll are in there, worth about eighty-five and a hundred and fifty grand each. I'd lay low with the Scroll for a while, though. Apparently, it's one of a kind.'

'You fitting me up?' asked Swingewood. 'Turned snitch?'

'No. If I turn snitch I go back to jail for Galliano and Malloy. Maybe Graham too. Like I said, I don't want any trouble.'

Swingewood opened the case. 'What about the *Dracula*?'

'It wasn't there. The other buyer must have taken it after I left.'

'Graham didn't say fuck all about that

50

when I phoned him,' said Acutt.

I shrugged. 'He had other first editions in the safe. Maybe he was going to do a deal.'

Swingewood frowned and closed the briefcase. 'What makes you think this is over.'

'Because I brought you the swag and you said you wanted an ex-copper on the payroll.' I pointed to Acutt and Tennant. 'So long as these two don't try to kill me again, and you don't ask me to kill anyone, I can live with that.'

'What about Galliano and Malloy? They were my men.'

I shrugged again. 'If they'd been better at their jobs, they'd be alive and I'd be dead.'

Swingewood glared at me for a few seconds. Then his frown eased and he smiled. 'Cheeky twat, like I said. Come on, gents.'

He picked up the briefcase and we all stood, just like on Thursday. Swingewood didn't try to distract me this time, though, and I followed them out and watched them walk away. When they were gone, I took out a pack of Gauloise, lit one up, and strolled along the canalside towards the bridge.

The options had been either go to war with Swingewood and lose, or let bygones be bygones and do a bit of semi-legitimate work for him as and when. Someone famous once wrote that you need a long spoon if you dine with the devil. It could have been Shakespeare. Or maybe Burns. I couldn't care less. My spoon had been long enough and I'd keep it that way next time I did business with Swingewood. Meanwhile, I had fifty grand's worth of Bram Stoker buried in the woods. My only regret was that I couldn't ask Charlotte to sell it for me. In fact, I couldn't even call her up to ask her out — far too risky.

While I was congratulating myself, I heard Dicky's footsteps behind me. I owed him one hell of an explanation. I started to turn — something cold and hard slid into my flesh.

I fell, hit my head on the tarmac, rolled onto my back. I felt something wet underneath me, and something sticky on one of my hands. I squinted and looked up at the sky.

The last thing I saw before losing consciousness was a tattoo of a pentagram and a mouth with two missing front teeth.

The Tired Captain

I remember the date very well. It was the afternoon of Wednesday the 9th August, 1893, when I received my first visitor in Baytown, where I had languished under house arrest for a little over five years. I'd been removed to the village of Robin Hood's Bay following an unsuccessful internment in a lunatic asylum in the seaside resort of Scarborough. My doctor had mercifully tired of seeing me in a straightjacket, and the relocation from under the shadow of the headland had improved both my mental and physical wellbeing dramatically. Indeed, I had not felt better since I left for the Northeast Frontier as a young man of eighteen, more than twenty years ago.

Despite my newfound health, I was bored beyond measure, and spent the majority of my time engaged in one of two pursuits. The first was writing a series of implausible adventure stories all too loosely based upon my experiences in the Metropolitan Police; the second was baiting the two disreputable detectives who'd been assigned as my jailers. Caine was an elderly ferret of a Yorkshireman, suspected of corruption to fund his gambling; McGinty was a gross, alcoholic young Munsterman. It was the former who disturbed my reverie on the day in question.

I had not slept well since the weekend and I was sitting in a deck chair on the little promenade next to Bay Bow, my prison. The sea was calm and the day clear, after the great storm earlier in the week. I was enjoying both my abstraction and the warmth of the sun when I saw the Yorkshireman approach. He stopped a few feet away from me; out of the corner of my eye I observed he was agitated, turning a calling card over and over in between the fingers of his right hand. I did not acknowledge his presence, but chose instead to play the game between captive and captor which we had come to learn so well.

Caine broke the silence first; he always

did. 'Mr Langham, there's a Russian gentleman to see you.' I looked up at him. 'I said there's a Russian gentleman to see you.'

'Yes, I believe you did.' I returned to my contemplation of the sea.

'But you're not allowed visitors — not unless they've been approved by the assistant commissioner — or it's the police surgeon.'

'Then send him away.'

Caine had four years left as my warder before his official retirement, and he was experienced enough to appreciate his good fortune in being allocated so comfortable a berth at the end of so inglorious a career. Though he would disappear to the races at York or Doncaster for days at a time, he was wary of making a decision which might jeopardise his pension. 'His card says he's private secretary to Count Brusilov, the Russian ambassador, and I don't want the count complaining to the commissioner, do I? See.' He offered me the evidence to examine.

The prospect of spending the rest of

56

the day on the second draft of *A Clue from the Deep* wasn't very appealing, but I had a role to play, so I let Caine squirm for a few seconds before accepting the card. It was made from the finest quality paper and embossed with gold lettering: *Captain Vladimir I. Gagarin, Private Secretary to The Right Honourable Count Brusilov*. Neither were known to me, but the arrival of such an eminent individual could only be related to the strange circumstances in which a Russian schooner had entered Whitby harbour, some six miles to the north, on Monday night.

I handed back the card. 'I shall see Captain Gagarin if you wish, but the decision is entirely your responsibility as are any consequences that may follow.' I turned away again, marvelling at the tranquillity of the ocean so soon after the raging tempest.

Caine hurried along to the cottage, muttering to himself.

A few minutes later, I espied McGinty lurching towards me, most likely summoned from the Nag's Head. I smelled him even before he opened his mouth to speak. 'Come along, Mr Langham, there's a foreign gent to see you.'

Though I was delighted at the change of routine, I affected a sigh as I rose from the chair. I followed McGinty to the sitting room of Bay Bow, and was highly amused when he stood to attention, swayed a little, and announced me.

'Mr Langham as requested, Sergeant.'

Caine was rubbing his hands together anxiously. 'Thank you, McGinty. Captain Gagarin, this is Mr Langham. Take as long as you need.'

Gagarin nodded once and the detectives left us. He was a tall, dark young man with a stiff bearing, handlebar moustache, and a long scar running down his right cheek. I deduced that he had served in the army rather than the navy, and attended a German university, possibly Heidelberg.

'Good day, Captain. Please make yourself comfortable and tell me how I may be of assistance to His Excellency in the matter of the *Demeter*.'

Gagarin's black eyes flickered, and his

mouth opened slightly. 'I . . . I prefer to stand.' His English was excellent except for a slight Bavarian inflection.

'As you wish.' I sat in the wing chair closest to the fireplace, and produced my clay pipe and pouch. 'May I offer you some tobacco?'

He shook his head. 'If you already know my business, then I have certainly found a most excellent agent. You will permit me to ask you some questions before I state my purpose?'

'Please proceed.'

As I prepared my pipe, Gagarin straightened even further, throwing his hands behind his back. He was nervous, and I suspected his errand was as sensitive as it was urgent. 'Thank you, sir. Do I have the honour of addressing Mr Roderick Langham, the former Chief Investigator of Scotland Yard who solved every case in which he was involved?'

'My rank was chief inspector and I had two failures early in my career, but I am the man you seek.'

'I believe you were dismissed in secret. May I ask the terms of your . . . situation?'

I paused to light the pipe and savoured the blast of tar at the back of my throat from the Ship's. 'I must point out that I was never dismissed and continue to draw my police salary, although my authority and duties have been revoked. In answer to your question: in theory, I may not leave Bay Bow except escorted by one of my warders, and may not leave Baytown unless accompanied by both. In practice, I am left to my own devices so long as I so not stay out overnight. The police surgeon is supposed to examine me every six months, but I have not seen him for over two years. I find myself none the worse for his neglect.'

'Your . . . health . . . has improved, sir?'

'I am still a maniac, but I have not had a violent episode for five years. My logical faculty seems unimpaired, though its exercise has been restricted to the trivial for half a decade.'

Gagarin cleared his throat. 'That your mental features are *par excellence* is obvious. Your confinement will not be an obstacle as I shall procure everything and everyone you require. I should therefore like to employ your services as a consultant on behalf of His Excellency, Count Brusilov, if you find such an arrangement agreeable.'

'I have a question of my own, Captain.'

'Yes, sir?'

'I was under the impression that my internment was known only to a small number of government officials, all of them British. How did you find me?'

'The Okhrana.'

The Tsar's secret police. I'd always known they'd had agents in London and had never trusted them. 'If the commission for Count Brusilov does not run contrary to the interests of my country, then I shall be glad to assist.'

'You have my word as an officer and a gentleman that it does not.'

'Then perhaps you will sit down and provide me with the relevant details.'

Gagarin sat, and slapped his hands on his thighs in relief. 'Aha! If you will tell me what you already know of the *Demeter*, it will prevent me from revisiting the ground you have already covered.'

'Very well. My knowledge stems from the lurid account in the *Dailygraph*, a somewhat more factual one in the *Whitby Gazette*, and a conversation with a coastguard named Skelton. Skelton maintains that the schooner had been floundering off the coast with all sails set for at least two days before the storm, and he is something of an expert when it comes to the sea. Regardless, during the storm on Monday night the *Demeter* was blown — or steered — into Whitby harbour, where it ran aground on the stretch of shingle known as Tate Hill Pier, under the East Cliff. The coastguard and police boarded the ship and found it devoid of any crew except the captain, who was dead, and had tied himself to the wheel. There are likely to be some legal complications in the Admiralty Court in relation to salvage, for a number of reasons, including the discovery of the tiller in a dead man's hand.'

'Your account is most accurate, with the exception of the hound.'

'Yes, I read about the giant dog, but didn't pay much heed. What was it supposed to have done . . . leaped off the ship and flown straight up the sheer East Cliff.'

Gagarin frowned. 'You do not believe in this hound?'

'It's possible, but I'm afraid you must take tales of black dogs with a pinch of salt in this part of England. The North Riding of Yorkshire is home to the barghest, the most ubiquitous of all of our hell hounds, said to roam from the Dales to the city of York, the coast at Kettleness, and dozens of other places. I'm sure there's something similar in Russian folklore.'

'Yes, I see. There is no . . . *bar-guest* . . . in my country, but the peasants believe in many evil spirits. The beast in question was, however, corporeal, as it savaged another dog to death later that night.'

I pulled on my pipe. 'Surely Count Brusilov doesn't want me to find the animal?'

'No, of course not. His Excellency's interest is in the ship's captain, Pyotr Ivanovich Romanov. Captain Romanov is a scion of the great House of Romanov, the family of His Imperial Highness, Tsar Alexander the Third. The relation is a distant one, and Captain Romanov's branch fell into misfortune several generations ago, but His Excellency is determined that his good name be preserved.'

'I don't think the count has anything to worry about. Skelton tells me Romanov is being hailed as a hero in Whitby.'

Gagarin reached into his reefer jacket and withdrew a sealed envelope. 'The inquest was held this morning and the log book examined, in addition to a document Captain Romanov had secured upon his person in a bottle. The log book was in order to August 4th, and reported nothing unusual except for the disappearance of the crew. The other document was more . . . of greater concern. I have made a translation for you. His Excellency returns to London today, but I am to attend Captain Romanov's funeral tomorrow morning and provide you with whatever assistance you require to resolve the mystery.'

'Count Brusilov would like the captain's name cleared?'

'His Excellency would like to know the truth, whatever it may be. I have high hopes for Captain Romanov's reputation, but should he have committed a crime — '

'The count would like to be the first to know.'

'You have it precisely.' Gagarin stood and handed me the envelope. 'I shall return after the funeral to take your instructions.'

★　★　★

On Gagarin's departure, I repaired to the book-closet I had established upstairs, next to my bedchamber. The room was tiny, with a small window affording a view of the houses piled atop each other on the cliff-side, but it was the only one available for use as a study. I removed the contents of the envelope, noted Gagarin's elegant hand, and examined the four sheets of paper at my leisure. Although the pages were clearly an addendum, Romanov had entitled it, *Log of the 'Demeter', Varna to*

Whitby. It began with a rather ominous sentence: *Written on 18 July, things so strange happening, that I shall keep accurate note henceforth until we land.*

The voyage had started without any such portents, at midday on the 6th July. The captain was accompanied by eight men: two mates, five crew, and a cook. Their freight was recorded as silver sand and boxes of earth. I wondered if this was as remarkable as it seemed and made a memorandum to ask Skelton. On the morning of the 16th July, while the schooner was in the Mediterranean, one of the hands was reported missing. Romanov wrote of a general feeling that someone or *something* was aboard. Sailors the world over are renowned for their superstitions, however, so I set little store by this. Despite dissent from Popescu, his first mate, the captain ordered a thorough search of the ship after one of the crew reported seeing a stranger aboard. Popescu was Roumanian, and unpopular with the Russian crew. Nothing was found, though I noted that the boxes of cargo were not opened.

On the 24th July, in the Bay of Biscay, another hand disappeared after going below. Five days later the second mate disappeared and Romanov and Popescu donned side arms as a safeguard. Their precaution was in vain as three more men went missing overnight. According to Romanov, this left only him, Popescu, and two other hands. I went back to the beginning and jotted down the numbers. The captain had evidently made a mistake somewhere, because he had started with eight crew and lost six, which should have left him with Popescu and one Russian hand. He must either have lost only two men on the 29th July, or had two remaining. Naturally, he was under extreme stress on the doomed voyage, but the miscalculation seemed unpardonable when it concerned the lives of his crew.

The three — or four — men were having serious problems sailing the schooner, which was now approaching Dover. Romanov had planned to signal for assistance, but was prevented from doing so by inclement weather. At midnight on the 2nd August he responded to a cry from the deck to find Popescu, and learn that he had lost another hand. Twenty-four hours later Romanov went to relieve the sole remaining hand, but he was also gone. I scribbled another memorandum and assumed that two rather than three men had gone missing on the 29th July, although Romanov may have been completely unhinged when he wrote the later entries in the addendum — he had already endured so much.

Shortly after Romanov took the helm, Popescu joined him. He was apparently deranged and claimed that he had attacked *It* — presumably the entity responsible for the deaths — with his knife, to no effect. He believed the creature was hiding in the boxes and returned below. Romanov's description of Popescu's insanity seemed to be confirmed by the latter's final actions. He flew from the hatchway, screaming in fear, and cried: He *is here. I know the secret now.* Then he recommended that Romanov join him, threw himself overboard. On the next day, the 4th August, Romanov wrote: *I saw it — him!* He made further reference to *this fiend or monster*, then tied himself to the tiller to make every last effort to bring his vessel safely in to port.

It was one of the most curious narratives I'd ever read, and a fascinating puzzle. First, I had to consider not only the accuracy of Gagarin's translation, but also his attention to detail. The secretary's English was almost perfect, but the discrepancy in the numbers of missing crew might have been his mistake rather than Romanov's. Second, if Romanov was a lunatic of some description, then I couldn't rely on a single word he'd written. However, the mention of a fiend wasn't necessarily proof of the captain's madness. By the 4th August he was physically, mentally, and morally exhausted, struggling on alone through the bad weather that had dogged the *Demeter* since the Bay of Biscay.

Throughout my career in the police I had relied upon the power of analysis, the science of deduction, and the calculus of probability, those three refinements of absolute logic so essential to the art of detection. Combined with some small skill in observation and a modest breadth of knowledge, my ability to reason had gained me the reputation which had brought Gagarin to my door. Indeed, so strong was my logical synthesis that I had been able to detect my own guilt in the crime which had ended my career, even though I was under the influence of an all-consuming mania, fuelled by alcohol. Now that my sanity and sobriety were restored, I had every hope of succeeding in a commission that fell under my own special province.

I took another look at yesterday's *Dailygraph* and read that Romanov had tied a crucifix and set of prayer beads to his wrist. Although it was illogical to believe in evil spirits, Romanov had taken rational steps to protect himself, and made a lucid and courageous decision to save his ship. No matter how sensible an individual Romanov may have been under normal circumstances, his final voyage had been a living hell, aside from which he was a sailor, susceptible to the superstitions of the sea at the best of times. On balance, I was inclined to believe that Romanov was not responsible for the deaths of his crew. He did not strike me as a madman — and I should know. Perhaps that was the count's real reason for employing my services, on the basis of setting a thief to catch a thief rather than my reputation as a police detective.

My cogitations were interrupted by Mrs Knaggs, the housekeeper, delivering the latest Dailygraph. The journalist, who went by the unlikely name of Kerr Bostam, was making a meal of his story, and had reprinted the entire contents of the captain's addendum by courtesy of an inspector from the Board of Trade. Bostam's own opinion was: *It almost seems as though the captain had been seized with some kind of mania before he had got well into blue water, and this had developed persistently throughout the voyage.* In fairness, he acceded that the public universally regarded Romanov was to be buried in the graveyard of St Mary's Church, on the East Cliff.

I also noted with annoyance that Bostam made two references to the

confounded dog before actually mention-
ing the verdict of the inquest, which
was open. There was nothing about the
cause of Romanov's death, which had
previously been reported as having
occurred within twenty-four hours of his
final entries in the log and addendum.
Exhaustion or excessive strain to his heart
seemed the most likely to me. Meanwhile,
the members of Whitby's S.P.C.A. — who
obviously had far too much time on their
hands — were apparently concerned for
the welfare of the mysterious hound,
despite the fact that it had ripped open
the throat and belly of a large mastiff. At
least such was Bostam's implication, the
story of the mastiff following close on
the heels of the *Demeter's* mascot. The
man was in fact relentless, writing of the
mourning over the fate of the animal
which *would, I believe be adopted by the
town.* What utter drivel.

I cast the newspaper down in disgust,
refilled my tobacco pouch, and went
outside. I found my deck chair exactly
where I'd left it on the promenade. A
certain restlessness had returned to the

sea in my absence, and tails of white foam were drifting on the breeze. A few miles to the south, I could see Peak House perched on a cliff. I was in good company for a madman: it was widely held that King George III had been treated there some three quarters of a century ago. I sat and smoked as I considered each possible sequence of events in relation to the evidence available, identifying the limited alternatives and narrowing down the solutions.

By the time the sun set I had constructed a hypothesis from which work, and with which I could present Gagarin. I was also soaked from the salty spray of the sea, which had lately begun to overwhelm the promenade. I carried my chair back to Bay Bow, walked past the Coastguard Station, and entered the Bay Hotel with the intention of finding Skelton.

★   ★   ★

Gagarin arrived at half-past one on Thursday afternoon and our business was once again conducted in the sitting room. From his sombre dress, I gathered he'd come directly from Romanov's funeral. He did not stand on ceremony: 'Have you reached a conclusion yet, Mr Langham?'

'No, but I have considered the evidence, and found a number of points that require either clarification or further investigation.'

'Please to continue.' He withdrew a notebook and a pencil from his coat.

'The man who murdered the crew must be one of Romanov, Popescu, or a stowaway.' I paused as Gagarin frowned.

'What about the search on July 16th.'

'You evidently know your facts, Captain, but the search did not include the cargo. It is possible that one or more of the boxes was not filled with earth and was used as a hiding place. The boxes were not search until the 3rd August, when Popescu opened an unspecified number immediately before his demise. I read in the newspaper that the cargo is in the hands of Mr S.F. Billington, a Whitby solicitor. I should like you to exert your influence to find out if it would have been possible for a man to conceal himself in any of these boxes.'

He nodded and made a note. 'I shall do it.'

'I am concerned about the state of Romanov's mind, particularly at the end of the voyage, when he must have been under an incredible amount of physical and psychological stress. I believe his mental state hinges upon one particular point which may be explained by your translation of the addendum.' I described the discrepancy in the numbers.

Gagarin made another note. 'Unfortunately, I do not have the originals in my possession. The police have retained them pending the Admiralty Court. I shall ask to see them this afternoon. The error may indeed be my own.'

'Thank you. I suspect that Romanov *was* in control of his faculties throughout, for however irrational his final entry may appear to us in the comfort of this cottage, there can be no doubt his behaviour was appropriate to the situation.'

Gagarin leaned forward. 'Could you explain this, please?'

'If we accept that Romanov was convinced he had evidence that some kind of murderous evil spirit killed seven of his crew and caused the eighth to commit suicide, then we must conclude that he took the necessary measures to protect himself from the evil and save his ship.'

'The evidence of Captain Romanov's rationality . . . is his reaction to an evil spirit. You are saying that there *was* an evil spirit?'

'No, I am saying that given the circumstances, it was not unreasonable for a sailor — even an educated one — to believe there was such a thing aboard. In addition to the precautions already described, Romanov even recorded the events in a separate document and took further measures to ensure that this would be available to whoever found the *Demeter*.

'Yes, you are right.'

'Let's leave the tired captain for a moment. I would like to speak to a very old sailor named Swales, who may be able to provide me with a more accurate account of the *Demeter's* arrival. I'm told he can usually be found with two of his shipmates in the graveyard on the East Cliff. They sit on a bench above the grave of a gentleman named George Canon.'

Gagarin sat up straight and regarded me with disapproval. 'This is an English jest, sir?'

'Certainly not. What makes you think so?'

'The man Swales was found dead this morning on the very bench you describe. I learned of it at Captain Romanov's funeral.'

'Was he indeed? What was the cause?'

'It is not clear, but I was told he was nearly one hundred years of age. I was also informed that he was found in the seat with his features distorted by a look of utmost fear. There was a curious incident at the funeral, but I suspect it is not significant for it concerns only a dog.'

I relented even as I groaned. 'Please proceed.'

'There was another old sailor sitting on the same bench with two most present-able young ladies. The sailor had brought his dog with him and the animal refused to sit next to them and began howling. It was so loud that it disturbed the priest and eventually the sailor kicked it and dragged it into place, on a gravestone. As soon as the dog reached the grave it stopped howling and started whimpering and shivering. In Russia, the peasants would say that the dog sensed the old man's spirit, which was still restless.' He shrugged. 'But it is of no consequence.'

'I think your peasants might say more than that. George Canon committed suicide in 1873.'

Gagarin smiled, for the first time in my presence. 'Aha! The grave of a suicide. The peasants say the *upir* lives there.'

I shook my head. 'What is an *oo-peer?*'

'An un-dead spirit of the Devil. They feed on the blood of men, and often take the form of a wolf. This is an amusing coincidence, yes?'

Perhaps Bostam would have thought so. 'While we're on the subject of these bloody hounds — damned and other — I have one more request. I'd like you to check the log of the *Demeter* to see if there were actually any animals taken aboard by the crew at all.' Gagarin made another note. 'My final question is about the inquest. Are the authorities completely sure that no one — other than the black dog — left the ship? Bearing in mind the chaos that must have reigned, and the fact that the vessel arrived at night, during one of the worst storms in years.'

Gagarin nodded. 'I understand your intention. The authorities have completely discounted the possibility. For myself, I also believe it highly unlikely. If that is all, I shall communicate the results of my inquiries as soon as they are complete.'

* * *

I received Gagarin's answers in a letter delivered by his manservant that evening. Although I was alone in the house, I took the missive up to my book-closet to read.

Sneaton Casle, August 10 1893
My dear Mr Langham
I have the following to report with

regard to the Demeter:

1. I have ascertained that of the seventeen boxes of earth opened by Popescu, all were a little over half full and contained enough space for a man to lie in. Furthermore, the lids of all fifty of the boxes have been perforated with small holes, which might allow a man to breathe. The evidence shows, however, that a man would not be able to release the lid from the inside.

2. Please accept my apology for the error in the addendum, which is in fact mine. Captain Romanov reported two disappearances on the night of July 29th, not three.

3. The ship's log does not report any live animals taken on board for the voyage.

His Excellency has recalled me to London, but any further assistance you may require can be procured from Mr S.F. Billington of Billington & Son, No. 7 The Crescent, Whitby, who has been retained by me for this purpose. May I ask that you dispatch the results of your investigation to me at the

embassy in Chesham place.
I remain, My dear Sir, Yours sincerely,
Vladimir Iosifovich Gagarin.

I suspected that I now had all the facts which I was likely to acquire at my disposal. I also had a premonition that the conclusion that must logically follow the premises I'd established would be disturbing. Maybe even paradoxical. As I sat back in my wicker chair, I heard the crashing of the waves against the sea wall below, a reminder of the half-remembered nightmares that had haunted my dreams before, during, and after the tempest. The breakers hurled themselves against the fragile stone and mortar as aberrant thoughts assailed my mind with equal vigour. I tried to keep my overactive imagination at bay by concentrating on my analytical skills.

Who murdered the Russian sailors?

I was prepared to discount Romanov, which left either Popescu or an unknown individual. In the latter instance, the culprit was required to have hidden in a box for ten days, opened it by means unknown, picked off the entire crew one by one even though they were alert to his presence, and then escaped undetected when the schooner ran aground. The offender must also necessarily have had suicidal tendencies to continue killing the crew in the ferocious weather. Homicidal mania itself was inconsistent with the sustained and calculated manner with which the crew had been despatched and discovery avoided. On reflection, I was inclined to regard the possibility of a stowaway as not only implausible, but absurd. My experiences as a detective had repeatedly taught me that the simplest explanation was invariably the most sound. There was thus no need to posit an unknown entity for which there was so little evidence when the facts appeared to incriminate Popescu.

I went through my hypothesis again, and once more arrived at Popescu as by far the most likely culprit. I picked up my fountain pen to communicate the same to Gagarin, but stopped.

I laughed to myself.

Popescu was the most likely of my

three suspects, but what if I included a fourth, an evil spirit of sorts like Gagarin's fairy tale shapechanger? I had already decided Romanov was sane. Perhaps Popescu was as well. If he *was* a murderer, driven by bloodthirsty xenophobia, why didn't he kill his captain? Romanov was no ordinary Russian, he was related to the nation's ruling family. The existence of a malevolent spirit actually fitted the facts of the case far better than a homicidal Popescu.

I laughed again, tittering uncontrollably — I couldn't help it.

The only illogical aspect of selecting the shapechanger over Popescu was the supernatural quality of the creature itself. I felt like Romanov tying himself to his doomed tiller as I reconsidered my explanation. Cast in this new, otherworldly light, everything described in the addendum made sense . . . and not just the incidents aboard the Demeter: the immense dog that leaped up the East Cliff, the coalman's dead dog, the dog on the suicide's grave, and maybe even old Swales.

That night I dreamed of barghests, dogs, hell hounds, and wolves.

Robin Hood's Bay, Aug. 11. 1893
My Dear Sir
I have the honour to present my findings following my investigation into the deaths of Captain Romanov and the crew of the Demeter.
I believe Captain Romanov had the misfortune to take on board a fiend of some sort, exactly as he described in the final entry of the addendum. I am unable to ascertain any particulars of the creature, except that it appears to have left the ship in the form of a giant dog and now reposes in the resting place of Mr George Canon, in the graveyard of St Mary's Church, in Whitby.
With the assurance of my high esteem and my appreciation of your own sterling efforts and assistance with regard to the case, I am, Captain Gagarin,

Very sincerely yours,
Roderick Langham.

I couldn't write that, could I?

If Brusilov took offence he'd have me back in a straitjacket in Scarborough before Caine could place his next bet. I probably deserved such a fate, but couldn't face it. The second paragraph of the letter I sent read:

Although it is likely to be impossible to verify the tragic events with complete certainty, I believe it is beyond a reasonable doubt that the first mate Popescu murdered the crew and then committed suicide in the early hours of the 4th August, exactly as surmised by Captain Romanov in the addendum.

★ ★ ★

The rain stopped shortly before dusk on Friday, so I took my pipe out to the promenade. I was faced with a dreadful dilemma. Either I had completely lost my reason years ago and could never be sure of myself again, or my morality was once more in question. I had deliberately presented Popescu as the villain of the piece. He may not have been a popular chap, but I think he was as brave as Romanov. He had first sought the evil out and then chosen a sailor's end over death at the hands of the Devil. Six years ago I had murdered an innocent man; now I had assassinated the character of an honourable one as well. Was there no end to my iniquity? I hoped Popescu had no kith and kin to be deceived by my lie, but even if he didn't, no man deserved to have his reputation besmirched in so brutal a fashion, let alone a brave man, and by a moral coward of dubious sanity.

I leaned against the rusted railing as I smoked, my hand trembling.

It could not be. If I *had* lost my reason, then my speculation about the shapechanger was invalid. There was no such thing as a shapechanger outside of fairy tales and Gothic romances, so I must be mad to conclude the existence of one. And if I was a maniac, then so was Popescu, homicidal where I was fanciful. For the first time in my wretched life I wanted to be mad, for if I was irrational all was well with the world. If my reason was intact, however, not only was I a coward, but the cosmic consequences were too horrible to contemplate. I *must* be a maniac . . . there were *no* shape-changers, *no* barghests, *no* Devils.

Suddenly, I sensed someone at my side.

I drew back from the railing and turned to see a tall, thin man with an aquiline nose and grey moustache. He stood mere inches away from me though I had not heard his approach. In the moonlight, his cruel face was so pale that I could see the veins underneath the skin. There was a scar on his forehead and his eyes looked as red as his thick, sensuous lips.

My jaw dropped open and my pipe fell from my mouth, breaking on the wet stone. I stared for a moment before regaining control.

The instant I closed my mouth he opened his. His nostrils dilated and he revealed large, white teeth, pointed like those of a beast. I didn't see him move, but felt the vice of his ice cold hand close on my throat. His grip was as strong as that of twenty men and I knew I was completely at his mercy. I froze in fear, losing control of my physical faculties. The fiend's hand locked against my jaw and he lifted me two feet from the ground in a single, swift motion.

I hung there petrified, suspended in the air by the hand of a dead man. He held all of my thirteen stone without any sign of strain, and even relaxed his grip enough to allow the blood to flow to my brain. I grimaced at his breath. It was like the smell of everything that had ever died — the ancient, the old, and the recently rotting — wafting into my mouth and up my nose. After what seemed like an eternity, he spoke in an accent from the Balkan reaches of the Austro-Hungarian Empire.

'You know who I am?'

I couldn't reply, but I tried to nod.

'The meaner things obey me, and sense my approach. Dogs and madmen. You have told the English about me, the Russians?'

I attempted to shake my head, then let go of his arms and waved to plead my innocence.

'I do not believe you.' He snarled and

swung me through the air.

He was going to throw me into the sea. I clung to his arm for dear life, but he cast me onto the walkway instead. Sprawled across the stone and quavering in terror, I squinted up at him, my teeth clamped, face rigid.

He smiled. 'But your friends will not believe you either and there has already been too much death in this place when I have many labours left.'

He raised his arm and I had not the courage to watch my own slaughter.

The *coup de grace* never came.

When I forced my eyes to open he was gone.

I stumbled back to Bay Bow and ransacked the rooms until I found one of McGinty's caches of gin.

For the first time in many years I drank myself into oblivion.

Meet El Presidente

Nobody wants to know about crooked coppers. Ex-crooked coppers are even further down the pecking order, so I was shitting myself about the summons to Filthy McNasty's on a Thursday. 'Fright Night at Filthy's' was so-called because the music downstairs was loud enough to stop anyone hearing you scream upstairs — and I'd only been out of hospital a week. I heard the bass thump as I crossed Amwell Street and checked my watch: ten past ten. The music stopped at eleven; there was still plenty of time to make me talk. I saw the two doormen through a small crowd of smokers clustered around the wooden benches on the sidewalk. One Caucasian, one Afro-Caribbean, both well over six foot.

'Evening, gents,' I said. 'My name's Farrow; Mr Swingewood's expecting me.'

'He's upstairs,' said Vanilla. 'Grace will show you.'

'Make sure you knock loud,' added Chocolate before moving aside to let me pass.

Assuming Grace was a woman rather than a religious reference, I entered the vestibule, and opened the wooden door on my left. The music was deafening inside, courtesy of 'D Bad Dog J', and the small pub was packed to capacity. Most of the punters were in their twenties or early thirties and dressed casual, except for a few tiny evening dresses.

I'm only five-eight, but I'm heavy and broad enough to struggle in crowds. I made it through the bar to the larger room at the rear, where the DJ was set up and dancers gyrated wildly. I noticed a tall woman dressed completely in black standing next to a door marked 'private'. She watched me as I approached, her hands crossed loosely in front, her back very straight. She looked like a taller, Mediterranean version of Jennifer Garner, and I might have paid her more attention if I hadn't been worried about imminent torture.

She returned my smile, and I asked, 'Grace?'

'You must be Farrow.'

'I am.'

'Upstairs, second door on the right. Come and see me when you're done.'

I wasn't sure what Grace meant, but the implication was that I'd be able to walk out — the first encouraging news I'd had since I picked up the message from Swingewood's enforcer. Grace opened the door. I smiled again, stepped into a narrow corridor, and ascended the stairs. I reached the landing, and heard raised voices from destination. I swallowed my fear, brushed a speck of lint from my cream suit, and thumped on the door.

Time to face the music — literally.

I couldn't believe what happened next.

The door was opened by a tall, pale man with fat cheeks, bad teeth, and greying blonde hair. Detective Inspector Moon. We'd met only once, when he'd arrested me for murder and subsequently released me without charge. As far as I knew, he was straight — I was obviously about to discover otherwise.

Moon held the door open without a word, I walked in, and he locked it behind me. The place was sparsely furnished: three wooden chairs, a small desk, and a large metal locker. Plastic sheeting covered the floor and thick black curtains the windows. Three of the other four men in the room were also Caucasian, and one of them was tied to a chair in the centre of the room, which was in turn bolted to the floor through the blue plastic. He was also naked with a bloody, swollen face.

Royston Swingewood turned to look at me. He was in his late forties, a stocky six-one, with a shaved head and calloused knuckles. He was dressed as usual, in a dark, tailored suit, white Oxford shirt without a tie, and Italian leather shoes. The suit jacket was draped over one of the chairs. He nodded to me and went back to work. His two top henchmen were with him. Tennant was a big Afro-Caribbean man with dreadlocks and a goatee; Acutt was slimmer and smaller, blonde with a dark tan. They were both wearing grey overalls and I noticed Acutt's suit on a hanger. We made a cosy group: I'd arrested Tennant and Moon had arrested me, zero convictions all round.

I stood with my hands behind my back, and Moon appeared at my left shoulder.

Acutt moved to the man in the chair, lifting his head up by the hair.

'It's not often we get an Old Etonian in the hot seat,' said Swingewood, 'but don't worry, I'm not going to hold that against you. The state of your teeth, though, they're fucking disgusting. I'm not going to hold that against you either. I can even understand how it makes good business sense to sell white and brown at public schools. The kids have money for the good stuff and you probably have a few connections still, right? Ah, kettle's boiling.'

The kettle on the table was indeed boiling, and the Old Etonian's teeth were indeed disgusting; they were black. There weren't any visible cups, but the bag of sugar and pair of diagonal pliers next to the kettle didn't bode well. Swingwood switched the kettle off, disconnected it, and opened the top. He poured some of the sugar in, replaced the top, and swirled the water around, keeping the kettle at arm's length.

The dealer started screaming. Acutt let him go and stepped out of the way. By the time Swingewood arrived in front of him, the man was straining against his bonds in a vain effort to try and curl himself into a ball. Swingewood tipped the kettle, and the boiling sugar water splashed down the man's forehead, face, ears, neck, shoulders, and chest. He closed his eyes and shrieked even louder, then shut his mouth as the liquid burnt his tongue. He grunted, moaned, and groaned through clenched teeth, spraying snot from his nose and pissing himself. When the kettle was empty, he gasped for breath before continuing to scream. Swingewood replaced the kettle, and leant his arse against the table.

I didn't move or speak. Neither did Moon.

The Old Etonian's skin turned pink and livid, and a patch on his scalp started to blister. He howled for another half minute, then started sobbing, keeping his eyes shut tight.

Swingewood picked up the pliers and nodded.

Acutt grabbed the dealer's hair again, punched him hard in the right ear, and said: 'Open your eyes, dickhead.'

He obeyed, and Swingewood blocked my view. 'Only, I didn't send my daughter to public school so she could end up a crack whore. You should've checked before you decided to set up shop. If you don't stop snivelling and listen, I'm gonna put the fucking kettle on again. Understand?'

The dealer stopped and tried to nod, but Acutt still had hold of his hair.

'That's better. Normally, after the warm up, I have Mr Tennant knock some teeth out, but I'd only be doing you a favour. We can move on to the next step, which involves permanent damage.' Swingwood raised the pliers.

The dealer was shaking uncontrollably as more skin on his face started to blister.

'I remove one nipple, two if I'm really hacked off; and I *am* really hacked off about some slag trying to sell gear at my daughter's school. If I see you again — anywhere — you'll be losing both.' He opened the pliers and snapped them shut.

'If you want to avoid that, I suggest you stay away from Hackney and Islington. But if I *ever* hear of you being within a mile of the City of London School for Girls, you'll pay for it in body parts — and I don't mean nipples. Selling well on the black market at the moment, they are. Understand?'

Swingewood took the pliers back to the desk, put his jacket on, and joined Moon and I. 'Take that halfwit back to his gaff in Putney,' he said to Tennant. 'No need to be gentle, either. And stay on the mobile; I might need you both later.'

Tennant nodded and Swingewood addressed me: 'I know you and DI Moon have met, so we'll move swiftly on. This noise drives me doolally.' He pushed past me, unlocked the door, and descended the steps.

I waited for Moon and then followed both of them out to a car park at the back of the pub.

Swingewood pressed a key fob, and a silver VW Phaeton responded. He threw me the keys. 'Drive.'

The Phaeton was about fifty grand's

worth of car, all leather upholstery inside. I climbed in and clipped on my seatbelt. Swingewood sat next to me, with Moon in the back. I started the engine, and switched on the headlights. 'Where to, Mr Swingewood?'

'King's Cross first. How's your back?'

'Fine thanks; the blade only nicked the kidney.' I pulled off slowly, indicated right, and drove out into Inglebert Street. I turned right again and headed north.

'Do you want me to find the twat and put him in the hot seat?'

'No thanks, I've dealt with it.' I hadn't, but I would.

'Good. You'll be doing any investigating I need from now on. Understand?'

'Yes, Mr Swingewood.'

'I've hired DI Moon as a consultant. He'll be your contact in the coppers. Be nice. Right now he's got a job for you, but I'm still the governor. Understand?'

'Yes, Mr Swingewood.'

'Moon.'

I turned left into Pentonville Road, and caught Moon's scowl in the mirror.

'Don't fuck this up, or I'll bury you.' I ignored him, and he continued. 'Juri Navratil is the current vice president of the Czech Republic. He lived in exile in Canada before the Velvet Revolution. Two years before, his son — Pavel — flew out for the first anti-communist demonstrations. He was last seen at a march in Prague in August eight-nine. At the time it was suspected that the secret police topped him, probably by accident. Ever since pops has been in a position to spend the Czech people's money, he's been searching for sonny. The search has recently been extended to include DNA databases. Guess what?'

I'm not the sharpest tool in the box, but I knew Moon was in the Met's Homicide and Serious Crime Command, and had been in Counter-Terrorism before that. 'Pavel's DNA has turned up at a crime scene in the UK, sometime after 1989.'

'You're not as thick as you look. Eleven years ago there was a double murder in Stoke Newington. DNA says Pavel was there. I found this out yesterday, and I won't be able to keep it quiet for long. You've got a week to find him, dead or alive.'

'Nothing more recent?'

'No. All the intel we have is on this memory stick.'

Said memory stick sailed through the air and landed on my lap. Pentonville Road and Gray's Inn Road merged into Euston. 'Why do you want me to find him?' I asked Moon.

'Because pops is offering a slice of the Czech Republic's GDP as a reward, and I won't be able to claim it as a hard-working servant of Her Majesty.'

'And what's your interest, Mr Swingewood?'

'I'm not sure yet, but it can't hurt to make friends in Eastern Europe. They hate the fucking Turks too.'

The appearance of drug dealers and prostitutes on the side streets heralded our arrival at King's Cross station.'

'Stop here,' said Moon.

I stopped the Phaeton. Moon said goodbye to Swingewood and left us. 'Where to now, Mr Swingewood?'

'My gaff. If the missus doesn't like you,

you're out on your ear. Grace has got a thing for you, by the way.'

*　*　*

At three o'clock that morning I retired to my narrowboat with a bottle of red and a pile of pages printed from Moon's memory stick. My back still ached and I'd been told to lay off the rough stuff for another three months, but there was no point in telling Swingewood that. He knew I'd picked up a little Czech and Polish in the Legion, so I had no excuse. Acutt and Tennant had already tried to kill me once. I had no doubt they'd succeed if Swingewood gave them another opportunity. I was just thankful that he didn't deal coke or heroin. Most of Swingewood's empire had been built from tobacco and alcohol smuggling, supplemented with a bit of illegal gambling, DVD piracy, and Ecstasy. His hatred of the Turks was practical rather than pathological: they shared the same turf in North London and occasionally someone died — usually one of them. I swallowed a couple of codeine tablets, filled my glass, put a pillow on the chair, and went to work.

Moon's dossier was thorough, with information from case files and Police National Computer reports, and a photo of Navratil dated the year of his disappearance. He was my age, forty, and had a cruel look about him. After his disappearance his DNA popped up on the radar in 1999, nine years ago. A couple of hairs from his head were found in a house in Stoke Newington where two Turkish Cypriots had been shot dead. Safak and Zafer Younan were brothers involved in prostitution, gambling, heroin, and human trafficking. They were both shot at point blank range with a nine mil by a person or persons unknown.

The closest the brothers Younan had come to having a legitimate business was an escort agency named Eva's Eastern Comfort in Farringdon Road. Upon their departure for a better place it had been bought by Elena Alexeyev, AKA Eva Alexeyev, who'd presumably been the pimp, madam, or whatever they called themselves. I flicked through for more information on her, but there was very little. She was Russian, had been born in 1959, and had lived in Archway at the time of the purchase. I'd need something more recent if I was going to find her.

I jotted down the details on a notepad, and thought about the situation some more. Navratil was obviously alive, or had been in 1999. His father had taken office two years later. Why didn't Navratil come forward then, if not before? The Czech president carried a lot more weight than his Western European counterparts, so even if Navratil had powerful enemies, his father would have been able to protect him. The only conclusion I could reach was that Navratil had stayed missing because he wanted to, which meant finding him was going to be difficult.

The painkillers and alcohol kicked in, and I started humming 'Meet El Presidente', one of the singles off Duran Duran's *Notorious* album. My taste in music is bogged down in the eighties, and *el presidente* keeps coming back to me. First there was a firearms drill in the

Legion, then a girlfriend's favourite cock-tail, and now Moon's vice-presidente. I lost focus as my mind went back to my close protection training. El Presidente, five targets at five metres distance. Hands on head to start. When the whistle blows, sweep left to right, one shot into each of the first four targets, a double-tap to the fifth, and four more on the way back. Change magazine after ten rounds and repeat. I could do the first half in four seconds, but I wasn't too hot on the maga-zine change.

Moon had provided his mobile number. I phoned and left a message requesting the current whereabouts of Elena Alexeyev. Then I finished the bottle of wine.

* * *

At half-one on Friday afternoon I was standing outside Mentone Mansions, a red-bricked Victorian terrace in Fulham Road, on the edge of Chelsea. I leant against the iron railing preventing pedes-trians from premature arrival at the two basement flats as I smoked my second

Gauloise of the day. Since my release from prison, I'd worked out it was a good way to remain unnoticed, because London was full of smokers exiled to the pavements. I was wearing a tie with my navy blue suit. I don't usually bother with the tie, but it added to my invisibility. I heard someone open the front door behind me. I dropped my fag, extinguished it with my shoe, and strolled into the apartment block as if I had every right to be there. The bloke on his way out didn't look twice.

I took the stairs to the third floor. I knew I was taking a chance on finding Elena in, and that she represented the slimmest of leads, but I had to try. It was either Elena or the Younan's associates, and I wasn't in any condition to intimidate Turkish gangsters. I rapped loudly on her door, and it was opened a few seconds later.

Elena was a couple of inches shorter than me, toned and shapely. She had long, tousled brown hair with blonde highlights and a perfect complexion. She sure as hell didn't look forty-nine. I would've guessed a well-preserved forty at the most, and that only from the few shallow lines around her cerise lips. She was dressed à la mode, in a white blouse, dark skirt, and high-heeled boots.

Tousled, cerise . . . focus.

'Ms Alexeyev?' I asked.

'Yes?'

'My name is Farrow, and I'd like to talk to you for a couple of minutes. I'll keep it quick.'

'You are not a cop?' She had an accent, but she'd obviously been living in England for a long time.

'No, I'm a private investigator.' You don't need a licence to be a nosy parker in the UK, so I was actually telling the truth.

'I have nothing to say.'

Elena swung the door closed, but I stopped it with my foot and held it open with my palm. Her brown eyes flashed with anger. 'Get out of here before I call the cops.'

'I'm sorry, but I need two minutes, no more. If you don't talk to me, I'll have to follow you around all day, and neither of us wants that. Just two minutes; I'll even stay out here if you like.'

She frowned, tossed her head, and opened the door. When I stepped inside the reception area she pointed to the lounge, which had a view of Fulham Road. The room was spacious, the size amplified by a minimum of furniture and decoration, and plenty of natural light through the bay window. The dark leather suite and solid walnut floor gave it a masculine feel at odds with Elena's appearance, and I wondered with whom she lived.

'Sit, but don't get too comfortable.'

I sat on the chair, she took the sofa. 'Are you the owner of Eva's Eastern Comfort in Farringdon Road?'

'No.'

'But you were in 1999?'

'Yes. I'm out of that life now.'

'I'm looking for a Czech man called Pavel Navratil. Do you know him?'

'No.'

'What about Safak and Zafer Younan?'

'Yes, they are both dead.'

'You used to work for them?'

'Yes.'

I shifted position to ease the ache in my

back and made a mental note to take more aspirin. 'I told you I'm not a cop. Navratil disappeared in Czechoslovakia in 1989; his father has been trying to find him ever since. Do you know who he is?'

'I've already said no.'

As much as I was enjoying the sound of her husky voice, I wasn't making any progress. 'I meant his father.'

'No, I don't know him or his father.'

'He's the vice-president of the Czech Republic. A very powerful man, and a very generous man where his long-lost son is concerned.' I paused, but she didn't say anything. 'I'll leave you my number so you can call me if you change your mind?'

'I don't know this man, so changing my mind won't help.' She looked even more unhappy with me than when I'd put my foot in the door. 'Your time is up.'

She'd said that before, I could tell. I nodded once, rose, and made for the door. As I turned the handle, Elena said: 'I'll take your card. I might want to give you a job one day.'

I turned back to her. 'I don't have a card.'

'Wait.' She disappeared into the lounge and returned with a pen and pad. 'Yes?'

I gave her my mobile number.

'Where can I find you?'

'The Globe Inn. It's a pub in Linslade, in Bedfordshire. What about your number?'

'Goodbye, Mr Farrow.'

I returned to my spot against the railings, lit another fag, and weighed up my options — or lack thereof. Elena knew more than she was saying, or she wouldn't have asked for my number. The line about a job was nonsense. She'd looked ready to go out to me; high-heeled boots weren't something you'd wear at home in a flat with wooden floors. I decided to follow her and see what happened. There wasn't any cover I could use except for a bus stop across the road. Elena might use it herself, but it would have to do. She was probably more likely to head for the nearest tube, which was in Fulham. The fact that she was a bit of a stunner would make it easier to keep an eye on her, though the tube could be a problem.

Twenty minutes after our conversation,

she walked out and headed into Chelsea. She didn't look at the bus stop, and I was confident my invisibility was working. I gave her a few seconds to get going, then followed. Soon both sides of Fulham Road were lined with shops, with the exception of the Chelsea and Westminster Hospital up ahead. As I reached the hospital, I saw Elena stride into Carluccio's Café. I slowed down, passed the hospital, and stopped outside a Starbucks. It's impossible to follow anyone on your own without running a high risk of either being made or losing them. I erred on the side of caution and ducked into the Starbucks.

I ordered an espresso and found a stool at the window as quickly as possible. I could only make out the entrance to Carluccio's when there weren't people or cars or busses in the way, but at least I was safely out of the way. Nonetheless, if Elena went back towards Mentone Mansions, I'd probably miss her. Fifteen minutes later she left the café and continued walking into Chelsea. I waited for her to pass on the opposite side of the road, gulped down my last mouthful of cold coffee, and followed.

I marched out into Fulham Road — straight into two men.

The big one held his palms up and pushed. The backs of his hands were covered in tattoos. The slim one had long, greasy hair and a tattoo at the base of his throat. 'Where are you going so fast?' he asked in a harsh Russian accent.

I rocked back slightly from the push, felt someone bump into me from behind. I half-turned; a youthful banker type with a mobile pressed to his ear glared at me from about a foot away. I grabbed his arm and propelled him into the smaller Russian. Then I used my forward momentum to drive my knee into the big bloke's crotch.

He grunted and pitched forward, knocking the other two aside. I took a long step to my right, cupped both hands, and clapped them together on his ears. Luckily for him, my right hand wasn't entirely on target. He bellowed, lost his balance, and went down in a heap with the banker.

The smaller Russian threw a right at me, but his centre of gravity was all over the place. I moved left, felt the air from his fist, and hit him with a left hook. My punch went up, over his shoulder, down the other side, and hammered his jaw line. He stumbled, tripped over the legs of the men on the pavement, and fell.

I was about to leg it, when I noticed the big Russian's wallet sticking out of his back pocket.

I snatched it, turned, and made myself scarce.

* * *

I gave the Russians — and the coppers, if they'd bothered — an hour to lose interest while I had a liquid lunch to steady my nerves. Two shots of Famous Grouse and two pints of Stella later, I took a window seat at Carluccio's, on the off-chance Elena would return the same way. I swallowed more aspirin with the espresso, and waited for my back to stop throbbing. I'd found two hundred and eighty quid's worth of compensation for my trouble from the Russian's wallet. I examined the remainder of my meagre spoils, a credit card and a Nectar card. I reckoned the former was probably false, but the latter might prove useful, strange as it seemed.

I made my second call to Moon.

'Have you found him yet?'

'No, but I've got a lead. I need a computer check on a Mr B. Smirnov. Like the vodka.' I rattled off the credit card number and bank details. 'I also need you to check a Nectar card.'

'A what?'

'You know — Nectar — as in a Sainsbury's, Debenhams loyalty card.'

'Are you taking the piss?'

'No. They both belong to the same bloke, but I don't trust the credit card.'

'Is there a name on the Nectar card?'

'Just a number.'

'Give it to me.'

I did. He hung up.

Time dragged. I could really have done with a Gauloise to ease its passing, but I didn't want to lose my seat. I settled for three more espressos over the next two hours instead. At least they balanced out my lunch. Moon finally rang back at five o'clock.

'What have you got?'

'Boris Smirnov and the name from the Nectar card, Dimitri Morozov, are both aliases used by Arseni Apraksin. Apraksin was born in Novosibirsk in 1975, currently lives in East Finchley, and was flagged up as a potential enforcer for the Russian Mafia after he was implicated in a murder in Tel Aviv three years ago. Do you want the address?'

'Yeah.' He gave it to me, but I didn't write it down. 'Anything else I should know about him?'

'He may work for a German telecoms millionaire called Vladimir Dragalina, who lives in Wimbledon. There was a scandal about Dragalina having worked for the Stasi during the Cold War a few months back, but otherwise he's a cleanskin.'

'*Vladimir* doesn't sound German to me.'

'He was born in Dresden, that's all I can tell you. Is Navratil dead or alive?'

My turn to hang up.

I was not happy. When I was a copper, the Russian Mafia were never an issue. Everyone knew they ran bookies, brothels, and smack, but it was always from a distance, at the very top of the food chain. On my patch in Islington they let the Turks and Pakistanis fight it out with Swingewood's boys, and never dirtied their hands. I'd never even heard of two Russians giving someone a hiding on the street. Maybe in New York or Tel Aviv, but not in London. *Stasi* was even worse news. In fact, ex-Stasi and current Russian Mafia was probably the scariest combination I could imagine. Unfortunately, it was too late to back out.

Five o'clock became six, then seven, and still my catwalk queen failed to appear. My patience expired at half-seven, and I joined the homeward bound crowds jostling their way to Fulham. When I reached Mentone House, I reverted to my earlier cunning plan. I'd not even lit the fag before someone breezed past me headed for the door. I gave them space, and slipped in behind.

I didn't think Elena was stupid enough to fall for the same trick twice, so I used a different knock this time, thumping hard on the door. After five of them, I leant all my weight against the door. There were a number of possibilities for what came next, several of which didn't bear thinking about.

I heard the click-clack of sexy boots.

Must play hell with the neighbours.

'Who is it?'

I put on my thickest Russian-cum-generic-Eastern-European accent and said, 'Boris.' With three names to choose from I knew my chances were slim.

I felt first one lock and then the next being opened — the door flew inwards, I followed.

Elena jumped back. I grabbed her waist, spun her around, and kicked the door closed behind me.

She shouted something in Russian and struggled violently, kicking and scratching.

'I don't want to hurt you, I just want to talk!'

Unconvinced, she threw her head back

— I barely avoided a broken nose. Her right heel lashed out — I was too quick again. Next her left hand, nails going for my eyes. Thankfully, my grip on her arms was tight.

Nice nails.

My momentary appreciation of her manicure earned me a boot heel on my big toe. 'Fuck! If you do that again, I'm going to slap you.'

Undeterred, she tried the same with her left foot.

Enough.

I lifted her whole body up, turned it slightly to the side, and limped into the lounge with my wriggling cargo. I dropped her on the sofa. 'Shut up for a minute, will you!'

She sat up straight, pushed her lovely chest out, and waved her finger at me. 'If you fuck with me, they will skin you alive. You understand what this means?'

I held up my hands. 'Yeah, I do, which is why I'm not going to. I won't touch you unless you kick me again.' She smiled as I hobbled to the chair, my kidney and right foot in agony. 'After our little chat I followed you to Carluccio's, and Boris and his pal jumped me. I know they're both Russian Mafia and I want to know what's going on.'

'When you left I phoned a man and told him what happened. He said he would take care of it. Grigori and Boris were supposed to warn you to keep away from me — and from Vlasta too. You must be good. They are very . . . *persuasive* men.'

'Who the hell is Vlasta?'

'Vlasta Blazek. You know him as Navratil.'

'He's alive?'

'Yes.'

'So why doesn't Vlasta want to be found?' She shrugged, but didn't answer. 'Don't you think that's strange? I mean his old man is vice-president. You'd think he'd want to go home and enjoy some of the perks.'

Elena laughed. 'I don't know what you mean by *perks*, but Vlasta is part of Dragalina's inner circle. Dragalina has much more power and more money than the vice-president of the Czech Republic.

You know who he is?'

'I've heard of him, yeah, and I think we should meet.'

She stopped laughing and clicked her fingers. 'Dragalina will steal your soul — just like that.'

Steal my soul? Creepy choice of words.

'I think he'll listen to me — unless he wants the coppers all over Navratil. I don't care who murdered the Younans, but the Czech left his DNA at the scene of the crime. Hair.' I touched my head to reinforce the point. 'The coppers know he was there, they know he's alive, and they're about to start looking for him. Dragalina will want to be told.'

'If you're lying to me, he'll eat us both alive. I mean really. He drinks blood and eats flesh. He is . . . *the devil*. I don't think you understand.'

I was relieved to be one of 'us' rather than 'them'. 'What, Dragalina's a cannibal?'

She nodded. 'Yes, like that. Many enemies have tried to kill him and they have all failed.'

'I get the picture. I'm not going to try

and kill him. I'm going to do him a favour. That's all.' Once again, I was telling the truth.

'I'll tell him what you say.' She paused for a moment. 'You could have hurt me and you didn't, so I am trying to help you. Grigori and Boris are nothing; if you cross Dragalina, he will bring you more suffering than you could dream in your worst nightmare.'

I nodded. 'I know the risks, and I appreciate the warning, but I still want to meet him. As soon as possible would be good.'

She stood. 'I will phone him now. Wait here.'

Yes, ma'am.

'You don't have anything to drink do you? Whisky — or vodka maybe, though I hate to stereotype.'

'Hate what?' She shook her head, her tresses bouncing off her shoulders. 'Through there, in the kitchen. I have whisky.'

I heard her speaking Russian on the phone as I poured myself a Ballantine's. I didn't like the sound of Dragalina or his taste in meat any more than the whole Stasi-mafia thing. I sank the first glass of whisky like there was no tomorrow — just in case there wasn't. Then I made my third call to Moon. I'd only been out of jail for a week before being put in hospital. This time, I was determined to stay out of both.

★ ★ ★

Noon next day I was walking up Globe Lane, a narrow service road leading from the canal to Stoke Road. With any luck, Moon would be waiting for me at the turning space at the top. I was humming 'Meet El Presidente' again, thinking about the cocktail this time, not the combat drill. Simona was a professional dancer and my most recent girlfriend. She'd left me when I was put away, and I'd not heard from her since. I'm not really a cocktail kind of bloke, but she'd got me into the El Presidente in the Bar Havana in Islington. The place suited her well, with her dusky Latin looks, although she was actually Romanian. She liked the

El Presidente with orange and no vermouth; I liked the works: rum, vermouth, and curaçao, with a bit of lime thrown in. I hadn't had one in years. If I survived the night, I'd go back to the Havana and drink a dozen.

Moon's Mercedes was parked facing the main road, with the engine running. I climbed in the passenger side.

He finished a call on his mobile. 'You're late.'

'What did you find out about Vlasta Blazek?' I asked.

'His first appearance in London was in 1991, which fits. He's alleged to have been involved in the big human trafficking ring that we busted a couple of years ago. Do you remember?'

'No.'

He guffawed, and his breath stank. 'Course not, you were banged up. All teenage girls — aged thirteen and up — from the Czech Republic, Romania, and Vietnam. They were locked away in houses in Bayswater, Highbury, and Manchester. Eleven arrests, four convictions, but no Blazek. You sure he's Navratil?'

'Yeah. Is that going to be a problem?'

'I couldn't give a shit if he's a convicted paedophile. When you find him I get paid, Swingewood gets another contact in the underworld, and you — well, who cares what you get. Anything else?'

'Just this.' I removed a black box about seven by three inches in size from where it was tucked under my belt. It bore the legend 'Security plus' in orange just under the electrodes. With my left hand I pushed it at Moon — catching him on the right forearm — and pressed the button.

He jerked as half a million volts shot through his body.

I removed the stun gun, twisted my hips to the right, and walloped him in the jaw with my right fist.

His head snapped back, his temple connecting the window.

I slid my right hand under his jacket and found the holster on his right hip. I unclipped it and withdrew the pistol, a Glock 17. I'd suspected as much.

Moon lost consciousness as I tucked the weapon into my belt.

I opened the door, debussed, and

chucked the stun gun into the bushes. I'd come back for it later. Then I crossed Stoke Road, and took a footpath for the train station up Knaves Hill. Moon would be compos mentis in a minute or two and I didn't want him coming after me in a rage. I'd have to beat him up and — much as I'd enjoy it — it would only complicate the situation.

I'd known Moon would be armed, because I knew he'd been involved in enough dodgy Counter-Terrorism operations to have a personal protection weapon. I needed a gun and I needed a copper's gun — because I knew it would work, and I didn't have time to test it. I'd taken the stun gun off some wanker who'd tried to use it on me at a domestic disturbance in Islington before I was nicked. I'd not bothered to charge him for it, guessing it would come in handy later.

★ ★ ★

It was a quarter to eleven on Saturday night, I was on Fulham Road again, and I was even more scared than I'd been on Fright Night. I slowed down and tried to calm myself. *Time to keep my wits about me . . . focus*. Either Navratil would make contact with his father, or he'd go underground. There would be no point in killing me, I was simply a messenger. Surely Dragalina would realise I wasn't worth the trouble? I was staking my life on the intelligence of a man I'd never met. I had dressed for business, in a beige suit without a tie this time. I didn't want to be seen sweating. As I approached Mentone Mansions, I performed the soldier's ritual, reaching under my jacket and touching the handle of the Glock. It sat against the small of my back, tucked into my belt, and the feel of the polymer gave me a little of the reassurance I craved.

The Glock is my handgun of choice for several reasons. First, it has an internal hammer, which means it can't catch on anything if you don't wear a holster. Second, it's designed to be carried one-up, without the safety, which is on the trigger. The safe action operates on a pre-set mechanism, so you can draw and fire immediately without worrying about accidental discharges. Third, the magazine holds seventeen rounds. I was hoping I wouldn't need any of them.

I took a deep breath, pressed Elena's buzzer, and waited.

From the intercom I heard, 'Yes?'

'It's Farrow.'

The lock buzzed and clicked; I opened the door, and walked up to the third floor. Elena was waiting for me. She was wearing a long, low-cut, figure-hugging navy dress. If I hadn't been so nervous, I'd have asked her out on the spot.

'I am not happy about this meeting,' she said.

I headed for the lounge. 'I'm sorry. Why did he choose your place?'

'It will not be for any good reason.' I sat down on the sofa. 'I will not offer you a drink. You'll need all your wits if we're both going to live.'

'Look, nothing's going to happen to *you*.'

Me, I'm not so sure about.

She spun on her heels and walked off.

Shoes this time, not boots, but still click-clacking away on the wood.

I wiggled my arse against the leather so I could feel the Glock.

Time passed. Slowly.

After what seemed like twenty minutes, but was actually two, I heard the buzzer from downstairs. The Russians — if it was them — were early. I stood up, forcing myself to take slow, deep breaths through my nose. Elena appeared in the foyer, spoke into the intercom, and held the door open. I retreated to a position where I would be out of the line of sight of anyone who wasn't in the room. My back was to the window and I was facing the door, with the kitchen on my left. I held my hands behind my back, felt the Glock under my jacket with the knuckles of my right hand.

I heard voices and took another deep breath.

Boris and a clone without a fat ear entered. Boris stood next to the kitchen door; the clone waited by the foyer. Boris betrayed absolutely no emotion, or even recognition. I heard the outer door close

127

and did not hear the click-clack of high heels, from which I deduced that Elena had been ordered to depart. Good for her, but bad for me. Still, I was glad she — at least — was going to survive the encounter. Grigori came in next, followed by Navratil, looking older and heavier than the photo I'd seen. Grigori stood next to Boris and Navratil next to the clone. The fifth man followed.

Dragalina was tall and slim with ivory skin. His hair was streaked with grey, and he had a thick, grey moustache, an aquiline nose, and fleshy lips. He was wearing a tailored black suit with a crimson tie; a matching handkerchief protruded from his pocket. He took a few steps into the room, so he was standing about three metres away from me, closer than his line of henchmen. His skin was so pale that I could see the veins underneath. He clasped his hands together in front of his chest, and his black eyes seemed to transfix me.

A line of sweat broke out on my forehead.

Dragalina looked at his watch — diamond encrusted — and spoke. 'You have sixty seconds to persuade me to let you live.'

His accent reminded me of Simona's. 'Pavel Navratil's father has had men looking for him since he became vice-president in the Czech Republic. A crooked copper I know identified Navratil's DNA at a crime scene in Stoke Newington in 1999. He hired me to find Navratil because he wants to be able to claim the reward. The copper knows that Navratil is Blazeck, but he doesn't know where he is. There are other men working for the vice-president, so it is only a matter of time before someone else matches the crime scene, Vlasta Blazek, and Pavel Navratil. I came to warn Navratil.'

Navratil swore in Czech.

'Very good,' said Dragalina. 'Very . . . *focused*.' He crossed his hands again. 'Why are you here?'

I felt a drop of sweat trickle under my collar.

'The man I work for is interested in the possibility of doing business with you. He sent me to warn Navratil as a show of good faith. He thinks it would be safer for him to . . . be somewhere else.'

Dragalina drew a deep breath, his nostrils distending. 'You may be right.' He had a brief exchange in Czech that I didn't understand, then he turned back to me. 'Navratil agrees with me, but he is not very happy. You have heard the expression *to shoot the messenger?*'

Here we go again.

Without moving my elbows, I gripped the butt of the Glock. I fought my fear and nodded slowly.

'You *have* done me a service, but I have everything I require and do not wish to communicate with your lord and master. You may go, on condition that you never make contact with me again, and do not interfere with my plans for Elena.'

I swallowed hard, throat like parchment. 'What plans?'

'She has betrayed me, so she will die. Her life for yours. It is the path of least resistance.'

My heart was thumping in my chest, blood pounding in my head. My vision began to narrow. 'I won't let you kill her.'

He shrugged. 'I will kill her — both of you if you insist, but you have thirty seconds to leave.' He looked at his watch again.

I didn't move.

If I live, I hope she's grateful.

Navratil moved his hand towards his chest.

Five men at less than five metres; ten rounds in four seconds. Weapon in hand for me; no mag change necessary. Start left, move right, double-tap, move back to the left.

Navratil's hand disappeared inside his jacket.

Go!

I drew the Glock and slid into the weaver stance, presenting a side-on target for the five of them. Everyone went for their guns. My first shot hit Boris in the chest, the second hit Grigori in the chest, the third missed Dragalina — even though he was right in front of me.

Navratil fired — too quickly — the bullet buzzed past my right ear. I shot him in the arm and hit the clone with the double-tap: face and chest, the bastard dropped like a stone. Navratil raised his pistol again — I shot him in the throat.

Dragalina — Dragalina wasn't there anymore.

He wasn't there.

I skipped him and shot Grigori in the chest. Boris had dropped to his knees. He fired wildly, a couple of metres to my left, into the wall and roof — I shot him through the top of the head.

I froze, waiting for Dragalina to pop up from behind the couch.

He didn't.

I peered through the smoke and stepped forward, bleeding and groaning men around me. No Dragalina — the front door was open.

How the hell?

The pounding of heart and head slowed.

I'm alive.

There didn't seem much point in leaving any witnesses, so I administered the coup de grace to Grigori, Navratil, and the clone. Boris was dead already.

Three rounds left; good old Glock.

I stepped into the foyer and fired a few

rounds into the wall opposite the front door to scare off any potential witnesses. Then I tucked the Glock back into my belt, and went to find Elena. I hit the stairs, started humming 'Meet El Presidente' again, and took out my mobile. Moon's choice was simple: either help Elena and I, or become a suspect in a quadruple homicide.

He was a DI in Homicide Command; I had his gun. He had no choice.

The Month of the Wolf

Some good luck, at last. I'm pretty sure the copy of Dracula I found in Scarborough this morning is a first edition. As is to be expected with my fortunes at the moment, however, every silver lining has a cloud. The bookshop, in Victoria Road, was a surreal experience in itself. There was hardly any attempt to organise the shelves and everything was covered in a thick layer of dust, including the proprietor with the mad- professor hair and his dog, which didn't move at all. It could have been dead for all I know — or care. At the rear, there was a sunken section filled with nineteenth century tomes. They were all damp and most of them were mouldy. The floor was actually matted with pages of books, stuck to the rotting carpet and trampled underfoot. Alas, it was here that I found the Dracula, without a cover, and with some of the endpapers missing. Had it been intact, I have a figure of £20K in my head, but in this condition it probably isn't worth any more than the £2 I paid. Still, considering that I've been put up in the corner room of the first floor of the Royal Hotel, it's a very good omen for my stay in Whitby. Apparently, my room used to be part of the upstairs lounge where Stoker came to write his notes for Dracula when he visited in 1890. A very good omen. No horror writer could ask for greater inspiration than to peruse a first edition of the novel — however abused — in the very place where Stoker wrote it. I feel fate has taken a hand here and I'm actually looking forward to doing my research this afternoon.

* * *

Anderssen stood in the graveyard, at the top of the famous hundred and ninety-nine steps, and looked at the West Cliff. He started to raise his fancy electro-optical system camera, but stopped, and turned around. He could just make out the jagged ruins of Whitby Abbey above the more prosaic parish church of St Mary's. Once again, he doubted he'd be able to replicate the success of *Norse Yorkshire: What the Vikings Saw*. The picture folio had briefly resuscitated his flagging career as a horror writer two years ago, but his name had already faded to black.

The gimmick had been original, but Anderssen wasn't convinced it was the sort of thing that would work a second time. He hadn't actually photographed any of the sites in the book; he'd taken photographs *from* them. The sites themselves — Jorvik, Cottam, and Scarborough — had been painted by his wife, as they would've looked at the time. He'd also exploited his Danish and Norwegian roots to claim 'authenticity'. This book would need another theme, another verity, and another illustrator, because Julie had left him for an artist. The bitch.

Anderssen scowled at the memory of his misfortune, and turned back to the West Cliff. He didn't have a choice anymore: he hadn't had a novel published in seven years, and hadn't even sold a short story in twelve months. He had to produce a book someone would buy, and he had to make the most of the weather. He'd almost run out of money, and there weren't many clear, calm days on the Yorkshire Coast in February.

He raised the camera and snapped away, moving from right to left, from the sea inland along the top of the cliff. There was the statue of Captain Cook, the whalebone arch, the imposing block of the Royal Hotel, and the tower of yet another church, all above the pier and promenade of the quaint stone quay. Further left, the houses and shops were staggered down the cliff face as the gradient eased, a charming historical vignette encroached upon by ugly, modern constructions. Anderssen swung back to the church. The monolith completely dominated the hotel and surrounding terraces, looming above them in a forbidding reminder of an unforgiving god. He snapped a few more shots, but couldn't zoom in because the other buildings obscured everything but the great tower.

Anderssen let the camera hang loose around his neck and looked at the West Cliff with his naked eyes. His *Viking* eyes as far as *Norse Yorkshire* readers were concerned. What a load of bullshit. The church commanded not only the surrounding buildings, but the whole west cliff, in much the same way as the Abbey on the East Cliff. It was curious that it wasn't advertised for tourists. Anderssen didn't even know its name. He switched the camera to standby and moved out the way of a small group straggling up the last of the stairs. The tourists were ruining his photo opportunities.

He was thinking about finding another vantage point from which to see more of the church, but hadn't yet decided if the Abbey was going to be one of his reverse-subjects. Although he'd been travelling up the East Coast, he'd driven from Scarborough to Pickering, and approached Whitby over the North York Moors. Driving up and down the hills and valleys, he'd realised that two landmarks dominated the panoramic view from the west: the ruins of the Abbey and Seaview Heights, a block of flats built in imitation of a Victorian folly. Anderssen wasn't sure whether he would use both of them, or only one, it would depend on what his as yet nonexistent illustrator had to say.

He was waiting for the tourists to piss off when he noticed an attractive woman sitting on a bench a few feet away from him. She was younger than him, early to mid thirties, and too voluptuous for his usual taste, but her chest was big and firm enough to hold his interest. Her black hair was windswept and her raspberry lipstick too bright, but her face was pretty, and her unpolished nails well-manicured. She wore a scarf and coat and was sketching one of the headstones in a pad, smiling as she worked. Anderssen's observations were interrupted when a fat man bumped into him. The tourist was laden with a camera and tripod, gasping for breath from the climb. Anderssen swore in reply to his apology, and returned his own camera to his satchel. Then he trotted down the uneven stone steps, his long legs and steady stride making light work of them.

He walked past the Duke of York public house, continued along the cobbled Church Street, and stopped at the post office. He browsed postcards with the intention of stealing an idea, but couldn't find anything worth copying. He spotted the *Whitby Gazette* as his attention wandered. It was an unimpressive little biweekly, but he bought one anyway. Anderssen hadn't only selected Whitby for its photographic possibilities, but also in the hope it might fuel his imagination. In earlier times it had been known as a writers' haven, with luminaries like Dickens, Tennyson, Collins, Gaskell, Stoker, and Machen all drawing inspiration from the setting. The Reverend Charles Dodgson, better known as Lewis Carroll, had even published two stories in the *Gazette*.

Anderssen realised he was hungry, and took the paper back to the Duke of York, where he ordered a pie and a pint. He sat on a bench in a bow window overlooking Tate Hill Pier and flicked through the

140

Gazette as he sipped his lager. There was very little of interest to a writer — or photographer — and the biggest news was the alleged presence of a panther that had killed livestock in Flamborough, Scalby, and Ruswarp. Anderssen had heard it all before; hoaxes, either deliberate or credulous. There was even a separate article about a local crank who claimed that Whitby was home to a werewolf. Apparently he was writing a book about it — self-published, no doubt. Anderssen stared at the pier and recalled that it was the scene of the arrival of the *Demeter* in *Dracula*, one of the most dramatic scenes in the whole book. He wished he could write something as impressive, but he just couldn't seem to find the words anymore. He was so desperate to keep writing he'd even started a journal. Somehow, it seemed like admitting defeat.

★　★　★

Whitby 'Werewolf' Claim
The recent sighting of an Alien Big Cat on the North Yorkshire coast has

prompted interest in another 'beast', which some claim to be a bear. Bears have been extinct in Britain for at least a thousand years, but there have been six reports of a large animal walking on its hind legs in the last five years. The most recent sighting was just after Christmas, by Pete Burgess, a driver with North Yorkshire County Council's Waste Management. He and his crew were picking up rubbish from a farm near Ravenscar when Burgess saw the creature coming towards him in the rear-view mirror. 'It were something I never seen before, big, hairy and black. I don't know what it were.' Burgess didn't wait to find out and drove off, leaving his crew behind. 'It had big pointed ears on top of its head. It could have been a bear, but it were skinnier. It were seven feet tall.' Burgess made a report to the Scarborough police, but they are not investigating.

Constable Mary Edwards, the Humberside Police wildlife officer, is currently in Whitby on the trail of the ABC, which was first seen near Hornsea. 'I don't think the Ravenscar incident is connected to my inquiry,' she said.

Local author Michael O. Brien believes the animal is a werewolf. 'I have been investigating and following it for five years,' said Brien. Brien claims he has received reports of dozens of sightings in this time, many of them close to his home in Whitby town centre. 'This is a phenomenon distinct from the barghest, I can assure you we are not talking about a ghost dog. I have proof that the creature is a werewolf and that it is nomadic, visiting the area two to three times a year. My hypothesis is that it is a female looking for a mate.' Brien's book on the subject, The Legend of the Whitby Werewolf is due for publication this summer. His work has spawned so much interest that he will be touring Yorkshire with the book. 'I already have two months worth of engagements, and I've had an offer to appear on Monsterquest on the History Channel in the States,' he added.

When Brien was asked about the proof, he replied, 'It's all in the book. You'll *have to wait till then.' Burgess's colleagues denied seeing anything, but Brien believes this is one of the most significant sightings, because it was both a close encounter and during the day. 'The details confirm what I already know.' Brien did not comment on whether he had seen the animal himself.*

★ ★ ★

The first person Anderssen noticed when he walked into the hotel lounge was the woman from St Mary's. She was sitting at a table on her own. He pretended he hadn't seen her and sidled over to the bar. When he darted a sly glance in her direction, he saw she was staring at him and smiling. Quickly, he turned away and ordered a double gin and tonic. He leant on the counter while he waited, playing it cool and hoping she'd appreciate his chiselled profile.

'Excuse me.'

Anderssen nearly jumped — the voice practically in his ear. 'Oh, hello,' he said, caught off-guard. He was startled by her proximity, and her wanton, lascivious expression.

'You're Felix Anderssen, aren't you? I'm Anna Salford-Bassett. I'm a big fan of your work, especially *The Footsteps at Spurn Dunes*. I think it's one of the best modern horror novels ever written.' Anderssen took her outstretched hand, but he didn't know what to say. 'You look surprised.'

Anderssen let go of her hand, a little quicker than intended. 'Astonished more like, but very pleased to meet you. I am Felix Anderssen, may I buy you a drink?'

'Perhaps later, I have a full one at my table. Will you join me?'

'Of course.' Anderssen gave the bartender his room number and followed Anna back to her table, taking a seat next to her. He noticed she wasn't wearing a wedding band and thought it was time to take charge of the situation. 'You must forgive me, Anna, but it's very rare that I meet a fan, rarer still that they're ladies, and even rarer that those ladies are alluring and intelligent.'

'I find that hard to believe, Felix,' she

replied. 'Cheers.' They touched glasses. 'I'm sure you're just being modest, but you might be surprised to know that I'm a professor of English literature.'

'Now I've heard it all! Are you sure you're talking about the same *Footsteps at Spurn Dunes*? Maybe someone else has written a decent one.'

'False modesty doesn't become you.'

'No, I'm serious. I lost my contract after *Made in Towton* and I've not been able to find a publisher since.' He shrugged and took another sip of his drink.

'I heard, but I'm sure you'll land on your feet again.' Anna grinned, revealing straight, white teeth.

This time there was no doubting what was on her mind, and Anderssen was convinced she even licked her lips surreptitiously. 'I hope so, but — I noticed you on the East Cliff this afternoon. I saw you sketching.'

'Did you? Yes, I'm on research leave this term and I'm preparing a paper on the gothic in literature and conducting some private research. I've just come up from Scarborough. I spent a couple of days at St Mary's there, under the castle, where Anne Brontë is buried. But I try and visit Whitby at least once a year. I feel like I can just smell the history buried here.'

'That's a coincidence,' said Anderssen. 'I was in Scarborough over the weekend myself. I've been doing a little tour of the east coast: Hornsea, Flamborough, Scarborough, and Whitby. I'll be staying here for a while though . . . ' He tailed off, hoping she'd volunteer the length of her own stay.

Anna placed her hand on his forearm. 'Ooh, following the ABC, are you? Or perhaps it's following *you*.'

'The cat thing terrorising livestock? Usual load of rubbish, isn't it?' She stroked his arm as she removed her hand, smiling and shrugging. 'Probably, but don't forget that there have been confirmed sighting of lynxes and pumas all over Britain since the Dangerous Wild Animals Act.'

'Oh, yes, I think I read about it somewhere. All these rich weirdos keeping cheetahs and leopards suddenly found themselves breaking the law, so they let them loose into the wild. But that was twenty-odd years ago, wasn't it?'

'Closer to thirty. You may be right, but I met a police officer from Hull this morning. She's hunting the ABC. She told me she was a dedicated wildlife officer, so the Humberside Police obviously take them seriously.'

'Seeing as Humberside is my local force, I'd rather they didn't. I'm sure my council tax could be put to better use. I'm afraid this whole big cat thing leaves me cold.'

'My real interest is in the ABC as a cultural phenomenon, as the modern version of the black dog of ancient folklore. Did you know that sixty percent of the thousands of sightings since 1827 have been big, *black* cats?'

'Is that important?' Notwithstanding the apparent potential to turn the encounter into a physical one, Anderssen was rapidly tiring of Anna's conversation. It had been much more interesting when it had been about him and his writing.

'The black dog has been associated

with death from the very earliest European mythology; the Celtic and Germanic legends subsequently evolved into the nocturnal spectre of more recent folklore, and have even spread to the States. The creature is a portent of death, often haunting gates and crossroads, and sometimes directly harmful. We're in the stomping ground of one of the nastiest, in fact.'

'Are we?' Anderssen asked without enthusiasm.

'Yes, the barghest, Yorkshire's very own black dog. It lives in a place called Troller's Gill in the Dales and travels as far as Leeds, York, Kettleness, and Robin Hood's Bay.'

Anderssen finished his drink in silent protest. He noticed her irises were amber in colour as he tried to calculate the percentage chance of her going to bed with him in the next forty-eight hours. Fifty. No, sixty-five. Overweight women usually had less confidence and less self-esteem, even if they were still attractive. Anything over thirty-three was worth pursuing. In fact, anything over twenty-five — his sex appeal seemed to have followed his writing into the abyss. Satisfied with the odds, Anderssen leant in so their faces were only inches apart, and said: 'Why don't you tell me all about it?'

No joy with Dr Salford-Bassett yet, and she won't tell me how long she's staying, the minx. Is she just another cock-tease or will she play doctor? I think she will, but with my luck, who can tell? Or maybe I should be thinking of her as a potential illustrator. Am I that desperate? I don't know. Probably. Meanwhile, I am being hounded (pardon the pun) by this ABC-black dog-thing. To begin with, Anna wouldn't shut up about its 'cultural significance deeply rooted in the psyche and shared memory of the European soul' (how people come up with this crap, I've no idea); then, as I was drifting off to sleep, I heard a loud, throaty howl from outside. Either someone nearby keeps a big (never mind 'black') dog they can't control, or per-haps the sound was carried on the wind. After half an hour of intermittent howl-ing, I gave up trying to sleep and flicked through my poor, battered Dracula.

I found two handwritten pages slipped inside. I've no way of knowing when they were written, but the paper is as discoloured as the pages of the book and the handwriting looks archaic to me, though the language used is modern English. A substantial part of the writing was too badly smudged by the bloody damp to be legible, but I was able to discern the following passage about an unidentified church:

. . . consecration ceremony led by the Reverend George Austen, a fearful and violent thunderstorm broke out, shaking the church and town. Suddenly, a black dog appeared in front of the rood screen lit by flashes of fire, and ran about the nave causing much fear and panic. Three of the parishioners were touched by the beast as they knelt in prayer for deliverance. Two were instantly killed and one was shrivelled up like a drawn purse. The hell hound then blasted through the doors on the south side of the building. Such is the tale told by the locals with whom I have spoken, although it seems that the real cause may have been the controversial phenomenon known as 'ball lightning'. If this is the case, however, the deaths should cause Lord Kelvin to reconsider his theory that the circumstance is in fact an illusionary one. The link to the Bargheust is hardly surprising . . .

More dogs! (But then it is 'the month of the wolf' — or 'month of bleak death' according to Dr Fox. I think I prefer 'month of the wolf'.) I couldn't read anymore because of the smudging, but perhaps I should think about incorporating the barghest into the Whitby project somehow. Something to ask her about, anyway. No more noise from outside, so I trust I'll be able to sleep after writing this (it's well past one o'clock). When I get up I intend to take a look at the Red Rock in Saltwick Bay and then the church on the West Cliff.

★   ★   ★

Anderssen spent Tuesday morning snapping photos of the sea, rocks, and cliffs in Saltwick Bay, but he was already having doubts as he climbed back up to St Mary's. The gimmick with *Norse Yorkshire* had relied on the geographical fact that many interesting historical sites are surrounded by more of the same. He could afford not to photograph the sites themselves, and rely on the novelty of the idea — photos *from* the site rather than *of* it — and Julie's skilful recreations of what the Vikings would actually have seen. Each of the reverse-subjects chosen had at least four places of interest nearby and the photographic canvas was filled with them rather than the sites that had already been photographed thousands of times. Whitby Abbey was old news, but if he could find three or four locations of historical interest in the area — and a decent artist — he might be able to pull off a sequel. He'd need a leitmotif too, but that could come later.

Anderssen paused in the graveyard and assessed the situation. The problem with the Abbey was that it was too near the cliff edge. The photos of Saltwick were adequate if not compelling, but that effectively ended the view east, and he couldn't fill up the book with pictures of the sea. There wasn't much visible up or down the coast, although there was an impressive viaduct inland, which he thought might still be used by the local steam train. Anderssen wondered if he could corner the trainspotter market, but he wasn't confident. He set off down to the steps again, his mood sinking with the altitude. His spirit ebbed to an all time low as he crossed the bridge and tramped up the West Cliff.

The curious thing about the Church of St Hilda was that it made less and less of an impression as Anderssen closed the distance. The view from the East Cliff had been awe-inspiring, the monolith towering above the houses at a malignant angle. There seemed to be something eerie about the construction that defied description, and he was reminded of what he'd tried — and failed — to achieve with his most successful novel, *The Horror Under Castle Hill*. He'd lost sight of the church at the bottom of the West Cliff, but it was still stark and overbearing when it had reappeared. Now, as he walked up Abbey Terrace to Church Square, it seemed almost ordinary.

He took more photos to make up for the sense of futility. The neo-gothic edifice wasn't anything special, and once he was standing opposite the building, it didn't even seem that high. Anderssen made a full circuit, capturing images of St Hilda's from all sides. He noted several intricate stained glass windows and wondered if the church would make a more atmospheric study from within. Both sets of doors were locked and the notice board only mentioned services on Sundays. He spent another fifteen minutes at his task before deciding to kill two birds with one stone at the Whitby Philosophical and Literary Society. The Society's premises were in Pannett Park and housed a museum, art gallery, library, and archives. The staff would be able to provide details on how to arrange a visit to the church, and he could search the archives for any interesting facts about it.

Anderssen's afternoon proved a total loss. He was given a name and number for contact at St Hilda's, but denied access to the archive as he hadn't booked in advance. He didn't want to book anything for tomorrow because more clear skies were predicted and he needed to make hay on the rare occasions the sun shone. He dialled the number on his mobile as he left the park — naturally, no one answered. Loath to waste time, he headed for Seaview Heights, desperate for a supplement to the Abbey.

The solid red brick square with its silly conical towers was another disappointment. It was actually closer to the sea than the Abbey, and lower, so the views it provided were fewer and more banal. Anderssen trudged off to Sneaton Castle for a cup of tea and a sandwich before finally admitting defeat. The 'castle' was no more impressive than the block of flats — in fact, less so. It was the Abbey or bust and it looked like bust unless he could unearth some colourful local history. He retraced his steps back into town as the sun set, disillusioned and defeated. He decided to rest his feet in Pannett Park. He found a bench near the flowerbeds at the entrance of the museum, and sat down, more weary in soul than body.

Anderssen made out the ruins of the Abbey in the moonlight, through the trees at the edge of the park. The night was cool and clear, but he'd never felt the cold particularly badly. Perhaps it was all that Viking blood coursing through his veins. The view of the ruins differed greatly from that of his hotel room, which was directly opposite, across the harbour mouth. Here, the Abbey seemed to be much further away, distorted somehow, and he reflected that things so often seemed more interesting from a distance. Anderssen was wondering what could have possessed anyone to build an eighty foot high telecommunications mast a few dozen feet away from the gothic ruins, when he noticed two pinpoints of red underneath the trees immediately in front of him.

He squinted, thinking they looked like phosphorous dots daubed on a tree trunk.

Underneath the red, he made out a rectangle of white, like ivory.

Anderssen felt an ice cold drop of sweat trickle down his spine.

Behind the eyes and fangs was a huge, black beast. Anderssen gripped the bench tight, frozen in fear. The animal was about forty feet away. Anderssen was sure it could cover the distance before he even stood up. His knuckles ached and his temples started to sweat. He heard a powerful, guttural growl, then the creature disappeared in a blur of blackness.

★   ★   ★

'More like a lion's roar?'

'Yes, that's exactly what it was like!' Anderssen and Anna were sharing a bottle of red in the hotel lounge, and sitting so close they were almost touching.

'I don't know if I should believe this from the man who wrote *The Church in Faxfleet* — one of the most astonishing debuts I've ever read, by the way.'

Anderssen raised his voice in exasperation. 'I knew you wouldn't believe me, but I told you I wasn't that interested yesterday, so why would I make it up?'

Anna stroked his forearm. 'Oh, I didn't mean to upset you, I'm sorry. If you say you saw it, then I'm sure you did. And of course, if it was an ABC, you're quite right, it would make exactly that type of sound rather than howling.'

'The howling . . . yeah, did you hear that dog last night as well?'

Anna removed her hand and drew back. 'No, what howling?'

'There was a dog baying for the better part of an hour after midnight, on and off. It stopped me sleeping. My room's just above us.' He pointed.

'I'm on the other side of the hotel, so maybe that's why I didn't hear it. It's curious that you use the terms 'howl' and 'bay' though.'

'Why?'

'Because dogs in the night tend to bark, don't they?'

Anderssen frowned. 'I never thought of that, but this wasn't barking, definitely not.'

'Do you think it could have been the ABC?' she asked.

159

'I don't know, it sounded like a big dog to me, but I'm no expert. What do you think I saw in the park?'

'From your description it sounds too big for anything other than a large leopard, even allowing for some inaccuracy brought about by fear — you must have been scared stiff.'

'Not really. I think it was more frightened of me.' Anderssen finished his glass of red, poured himself another, and topped up Anna's glass without asking.

'Thank you.'

'I thought leopards were yellow with spots — as in *can't change*?'

'They are, but there are melanistic and leucistic variants, commonly called black and white panthers, but really just leopards with either too much or too little pigmentation. The spots are still there, they're just harder to see.'

'Whatever it is, I hope it doesn't come too close. Cat hair gives me hayfever, and it looked like it had a lot of hair. Having said that, though, meeting your ABC was the highlight of my day.'

'That bad, hey?'

'I fear so. With your interest in the gothic, I don't suppose you know anything about St Hilda's — the church, not the Abbey.'

'A little.'

'I'm considering including it in my pictorial study. Is there anything interesting or unusual in its history?'

'Very much so. It's supposed to be cursed. What I find really interesting is that it became the focus of the barghest legend in Whitby when it was built in 1888.'

'Even though black dog legends are thousands of years old?'

'That's why it's so interesting. You see Whitby's barghest comes from the ninth century Viking attack that destroyed the Abbey. Apparently there was a particularly nasty war dog that accompanied the Saxon warriors who defended the monastery. They couldn't hold off the Vikings and most of them — along with the dog — were killed. The dog's spirit was restless because it had failed to defend the holy ground, and haunted the East Cliff. But in the last hundred years, he

161

jumped across the river and is now associated with the West Cliff as far up as Kettleness.'

'What about the warriors,' Anderssen asked, 'do they still haunt the East Cliff?'

Anna's tongue appeared between her lips, her lips, tongue, and teeth stained red from the wine. Anderssen found himself strangely aroused by the sight. 'No, but that's the resonance of the black dog in the collective unconscious for you.'

Before she started with her cultural significance nonsense, he thought it was time to try and find other uses for that blood red mouth. 'How long are you staying for?'

★   ★   ★

13 Feb
What started as a bad day with lack of sleep got worse and worse, hitting a low point when a melanistic leopard scared the crap out of me in the park . . . long story. However, all's well that ends well, or so it seems. In another unsuccessful attempt to seduce Anna, I asked to see her sketches of the Abbey.

162

They were excellent, and without thinking I asked if she'd consider collaborating with me on the book. (I can always drop her later if I find someone better.) She wouldn't commit, but I could see she was interested. Tomorrow night she's going to sketch the Abbey from the West Cliff if the rain holds off, and I'm going to meet her at the whalebone arch at midnight. Midnight! She said something about the view, but I didn't fall for that. Looks like I'm finally 'in', though it's the sketches I'm after at the moment.

What with all this barghest nonsense, I reread the chapter in Dracula where the Demeter arrives in Whitby. Stoker really had a knack for high drama — perhaps from his day-job as a theatre manager — and it really is a gripping read. In the midst of a raging storm the high seas toss the ship from the mist, and it flies headlong into the harbour, a dead man lashed to the wheel . . . as soon as the schooner runs aground on the gravel, 'an immense dog' leaps ashore and disappears up the East Cliff. Hah, potent stuff!

I wonder if Anna is right and Stoker did get the idea from the legends about the barghest in Whitby. Perhaps the dog running up to the Abbey is significant? I wonder what he thought about the Church of St Hilda when he was here.

★ ★ ★

There was only the faintest hint of moonlight visible from behind the Abbey when Anderssen left the Royal Hotel five minutes before midnight. He'd deliberately avoided the hotel bar and restaurant that evening — so as to whet Anna's appetite for all manner of collaborations — and dressed carefully in a brown leather jacket, black polo neck, and olive cords. He'd shaved and brushed his teeth before spending some time in front of the mirror. It was only a few dozen paces from the Royal to the end of the West Cliff, which was dominated by the statue of Cook. There were several benches arranged around the monument and the south and eastern edges of the cliff, and he expected to find Anna on one of these.

She wasn't. Anderssen thought she was probably practicing a fashionable tardiness. He stood alone on the paved square, enjoying the clear, cold night. He didn't mind waiting, not when he knew it was a sure thing. He looked through the whalebone arch across the harbour, to St Mary's and the Abbey, perfectly framed by the two rib bones of a great beast. He'd already taken a few photos of the view, even though the Abbey wasn't likely to feature in the folio. Anderssen glanced to his right to see if Anna was on her way from the hotel, and his peripheral vision caught movement to the front. There was a lamp on the other side of the arch, where the path disappeared down to the West Pier. He saw a shadow at the edge of the light, or below it. He blinked and realised he was looking at a dustbin.

He chuckled to himself, turned back to the hotel — the dustbin moved.

The forequarters of a huge animal emerged from behind the dustbin, pawing up the path towards him.

Anderssen froze.

The creature closed on him, padding

with perfect balance. It was jet black, with smouldering red eyes as big as saucers. It looked like an enormous hound, and moved like a cat, back arched, paws barely touching the ground. It stopped in the arch, less than ten feet away.

Anderssen shivered uncontrollably, his feet rooted to the spot. The monster's head was the same height as his sternum and it had a massive chest and slim hindquarters. It bared its huge white fangs and let out a stentorian growl. Then it passed under the arch and moved to Anderssen's right, cutting off his line of retreat.

He was so scared he hadn't even taken his hands out of his pockets. The beat of his heart thumped in his head, cold sweat drenched his body. His teeth chattered as his muscles convulsed, and he would have emptied his bladder had he not just done so in preparation for his assignation. With a supreme effort, Anderssen managed to turn on his heels and follow the beast as it stalked a semi-circle around him.

When it was behind him, it growled again, louder, then roared like thunder.

Anderssen dropped to his knees. The hellhound lowered its head, fixed him with eyes of fire, and advanced.

The stink of fetid breath and wet dog hair was overpowering, but Anderssen didn't have the physical or mental strength to fight or flee. When the mist from the beast's maw mixed with that of his own body, he shut his eyes, unable and unwilling to watch his own end. If nothing else, he would die without having to see the monster again. That would be more than he could bear. Anderssen started sobbing, the tears mixing with his sweat.

Some time later, he realised the smell was fading. Anderssen opened his eyes and saw he was alone on the cliff top.

He screamed, and didn't stop until the police arrived.

★   ★   ★

15 Feb
I've worked the whole thing out! It's a ghost, not a real dog — or cat, or anything. Yes, I saw and heard and smelled it, but it can't physically harm

me. *How do I know? I'm allergic to cat hairs and dog dander! If a cat or dog the size of a cow came close enough to lick my face, I'd be sneezing and crying for hours. I didn't even sniff. Maybe it was the adrenalin and the fear, but I doubt it. It isn't real. All it can do is scare me! That's probably why it circled, to try and get me to run off the cliff or something clichéd like that. But I know the truth now: it can't touch me. There's nothing it can do.*

I worked out the rest, as well. I think these notes inside my Dracula are Stoker's. I think he's referring to the Church of St Hilda and that's where he got his idea about Dracula and the dog from. Anna said it was cursed, and I'll bet that's why — because of what happened at the consecration ceremony. The dates fit perfectly, and Stoker spoke with the locals when he researched his novel.

Tonight, I'm going to break into the church and take a look for myself.

As for Anna, I don't know where she is. I haven't seen her since Tuesday night.

I'm not interested in her or her sketches, though. It's the barghest I'm after. I can hear it howling now. I'm going to conquer my fear, find its lair, and tame the beast. Then I'm going to write about the whole thing. Fiction and non-fiction — the works. Monsterquest, the History Channel, I'll be a household name by next week. All my books will be back in print, there'll be options for movies, and I'll have my pick of agents. Brilliant! This is it — my luck has changed — coming to Whitby was the right thing to do. Fate. Personal destiny. What did my ancestors call it? Something like the wyrd or weird. I can't remember, but all I have to do is find the dog in the church.

Child's play.

A small price to pay.

Archaeological Find in
St Hilda's Church

Following the recent tragedy, Canon Tim Alston agreed to have the flagstone in front of the pulpit in St Hilda's Church raised. The request came from Professor Anna Salford-Bassett, an expert in cultural history from Bristol University, who is a regular visitor to Whitby. The excavation was performed on Wednesday, and the bones of a dog and a man were found in a hollow beneath, intertwined. The dog's jaws were locked around the man's throat and a pattern-welded sword lay in between the dog's ribs. Dr Daniel Gustafson, an archaeologist from the University of York, dated the remains to the ninth century, and described the sword as of Viking origin. Last week, Felix Anderssen, a retired author from Beverley, was discovered sitting in the bishop's chair, stark naked, and raving about the barghest. He became violent when the police arrived and has since been sectioned under the provisions of the Mental Health Act. Professor Salford-Bassett, who knew Anderssen, said that she had been concerned for his safety, and that he had told her that it was his ancestral duty to destroy the Saxon dog.

Blue Mail

Nobody likes a crooked copper. It didn't matter that I wasn't crooked before I went to prison, it was enough that I'd been crooked since. With a single exception my former colleagues despised me more than my former enemies, which was how I came to be walking along the cobbles of Fore Street in St Ives. I could see the shop I wanted up ahead, through the throngs of holidaymakers enjoying what passed for a British summer at the seaside. It was gone six and 'Elliott and Son, Gentlemen's Outfitters', was closed. I knocked anyway.

Nothing, nor could I make out any sign of life inside. I banged the glass door again, harder this time, and double-checked my Tag Heuer. Someone should still be here. I raised my fist again, but stopped when I saw a small man limping towards me. He was short — five and a half foot at the most — and bald on top, with a white tonsure and tash, both neatly trimmed. I guessed he was around fifty-five, but I couldn't be sure because his little round face had a weather-beaten look, from too much sun and wind. As soon as he had the door open, he smiled, revealing a sparkling set of false teeth.

'I'm sorry, sir, we're closed.' His eyes fixed on my Ungaro suit, worn without a tie. 'Not bad, but a tailored double-breasted jacket would look so much better, particularly for a gentleman with your physique. Perhaps you could come back tomorrow and I can show you what I have in stock?'

I'm only five-eight, but I weight two hundred and ten pounds and not much of it is fat. 'Are you Brendan Elliott?' I asked.

'I am.'

'My name's Farrow. Mr Swingewood sent me.'

'Ah, yes, of course. I should have realised; how stupid of me. Please come in.' He locked the door behind me. 'I've sent all my staff home, so this is the best place, to talk, if you've no objection?' I shrugged, and he led me across the shop floor, through a door marked 'private', and into a small office at the rear of the premises. 'I was just cashing up. Please sit down. Would you like a glass of whisky? It's Jameson.'

There was a bottle and a near-empty glass on the desktop, along with cash, receipts, and a counting machine. 'If you don't mind, I'd rather get straight down to business. Mr Swingewood seems to think you need help, and that I'm the right man for the job.'

I had an uneasy alliance with Royston Swingewood, a Hackney villain, and did some of his legitimate work for him. All he'd told me about his cousin was that he was from the straight side of the family.

'Yes, I certainly hope so.' Elliott had a slight lisp. 'I have a son,' he said, as if that explained everything. 'Not a bad lad, but this isn't the first time I've had to bail him out of trouble. He's an actor — done quite well for himself on the stage and in TV — and he's busy filming his first Hollywood feature. The first of many, we both hope.'

Elliott paused again, but I said nothing.

I didn't give any of those encouraging non-verbal cues either.

He gulped down some whisky.

'Yes, well. He met a young woman a couple of months ago, they had a brief affair, and then last week she sent him a photograph of the two of them together — *on the nest*, one might say. She wants twenty-five thousand pounds for the full set of photos.'

'Is he married?' I asked.

'No.'

'I don't get it.'

'I'm not sure I understand.'

'That's what I said. Your son isn't a celebrity yet. Who gives a shit if he gets photographed on the job?'

'Well, the problem is that the film is *The Voyage of the 'Dawn Treader'*, the next Narnia. It's for children,' he added in response to my blank look. 'My son is concerned that if he appears in the flesh in the News of the World, the director might drop him, seeing as he can be replaced.'

There's always a career in porn, I

thought. 'Do you have the money?'

'He sent it to me. It is, in fact, exactly what he's being paid for the film. His lady-friend knew what she was doing.'

I whistled. 'I hope she was a good shag. What do you want me to do?'

'Meet me at the bank when I draw the money and keep me company when I do the exchange. The lady in question appears to be in league with a man named Murrin, from Camborne. He's small time by your London standards, but he pretty much runs this part of Cornwall. I'm meeting him outside the Engine Inn, in Nancledra, at noon tomorrow. Could you meet me at the Barclays Bank in Bedford Road at half-eleven?'

'Yeah, I'm at Tregenna Castle if you need me.'

★　★　★

I was five minutes early, but Elliott was already waiting in the foyer of the bank, with a slim leather briefcase clenched tight in his right fist. He hung on to it as he limped up the hill to his car, a grey Jaguar XJ sport. Once we were both inside, he handed me the case, and I put it on the floor between my feet. We were silent as he negotiated the traffic up to the Penzance road. It took ten minutes to leave the town, but then our progress was quicker. A few hundred metres beyond the hamlet of Cripplesease, Elliott pulled into the car park of the Engine Inn. There were half a dozen vehicles there already, but not the one we were expecting.

'Do you want me to make the exchange when they turn up?' I asked.

'No, I'll do that, but I'd like you to get out of the car and . . . well, I don't know, just look tough. Perhaps you could put your hands inside your coat as if you're armed. Something like that.'

'I am armed.'

'Oh. Er, good.'

Five minutes later a dark blue BMW drove in at speed, and skidded to a halt about fifteen metres away. There were two occupants, both giants. They looked at us, made the connection, and switched off the engine. I did what Elliott had asked, walking around the driver's side of the Jag, and leaning against the bonnet. He took the briefcase and joined me. I folded my arms and watched the two Cornish pasties pour from the B-M.

They were enormous, both over six foot and three hundred pounds. Fat fuckers, but you still wouldn't want to get up close and personal with them. One was young, mid-twenties, crew-cut and clean-shaven; the other ten years older, balding with a goatee. They were both wearing long leather coats, which seemed ominous, given that it was another bright and blustery summer's day.

I reached around to the small of my back, where my Taurus .38 Special was sitting snug in a holster clipped on the inside of my belt. I put my right hand around the rubber grip and my left on the bonnet, so it looked like I was propping myself up.

Fat Boy and Fat Man stood either side of the B-M, facing us. Fat Boy glared at me and mumbled something to his mate. Fat Man opened the back door of the car and reached inside.

I tensed and drew the Taurus from the holster, keeping it out of sight behind me.

Fat Man straightened up with a briefcase in his hand, a chunky black one. He waved at Elliott. 'Come on, then.'

Elliott cleared his throat and walked across the car park. He exchanged briefcases with Fat Man, who absolutely dwarfed him, and then came back. Fat Boy followed him.

'You'd better check the goods,' I said.

'I know.' He popped the boot and went to the back of the Jag.

I wanted to put the Taurus away so I could use both hands if Fat Boy turned nasty, but the problem with inside holsters is that you have to take them off to put your weapon away. As the revolver only had a two inch barrel, I kept hold of it, slipping the front into my trouser pocket, and concealing the rest with my hand.

Fat Boy had both his hands in the pockets of his flash coat. He stopped about a foot away from me. 'The fuck are you?'

Several witty rejoinders came to mind.

178

'Someone you'll never see again.'

'Dunno about that. You're keeping the wrong company, cos this aint over.'

I heard the boot slam shut and Elliott's voice: 'That's it, we can leave.'

'Not till we say so,' said Fat Boy.

I glanced at Elliott, who sat back in the car.

'Where you from?'

'Lots of different places,' I replied.

Fat Man shouted from the car: 'Tommy, leave him.'

Fat Boy glared at me one last time, hawked, and spat on my right shoe. Then he walked back to the B-M, which sunk closer to the ground when he squeezed in. Fat Man reversed, hit his brakes, and shot off onto the road. His passenger flipped me the bird.

When they were gone, I resumed my seat next to Elliott. 'You got the photos?'

'All there.'

'And the negatives?'

'Everything. You were perfect, thank you. How much do I owe you?'

'Nothing. Mr Swingewood's taking care of it.'

Elliott started the car, and we set off back to St Ives. 'Something wrong?' he asked.

I shook my head, but I was wondering about Fat Boy. Was he another sociopath in the making, or had someone ruffled his feathers prior to our meeting? I decided to stick around instead of going straight back to London. Swingewood had paid well, Tregenna Castle was lovely, and one of the other guests was the spitting image of Keira Knightley.

*　*　*

Twenty-four hours later, I was soaking up the sun on a recliner, in my swimming trunks and a pair of dark glasses. The majority of the residents had made the most of a rare idyllic day by relocating to the beaches; a few of us preferred the poolside. Regrettably, there was no sign of Keira, but I had cold lager on the table next to me, and I was reading a T.E.D. Klein anthology, so it wasn't all bad.

A shadow fell over me and the man blocking my sunlight said: 'Farrow.' He was in his mid-forties, tall and heavily built, with short grey hair and a neat moustache. He was wearing a lightweight leather jacket, open-necked Oxford shirt, chinos, and expensive shoes. He slouched with his hands in his pockets and his head cocked at a strange angle.

'Yeah.'

'My name's Murrin.'

I pulled the back of the recliner up and said, 'Make yourself comfortable.'

He took a seat in the shade and placed a pack of Regals and a gold zippo on the table. His hands were huge. He lit a fag and blew the smoke into the sea breeze.

When he said nothing, I asked, 'What can I do for you, Mr Murrin?'

He laughed and had another pull on his fag. 'If you know who I am, why do you think you're still alive?'

I reached for my pack of Gauloise and fired up. 'Because I've not done anything to piss you off?'

'Funny. You're still here sitting in the sun smoking those disgusting cigarettes because: one, I know who you work for; and two, I know who Elliott is. You follow?'

I didn't. 'No.'

'You winding me up?'

'I'm well aware of who you are. I did Elliott a favour at Mr Swingewood's request, made sure your boys didn't lean on him too hard. He got what he was after, you got your money; I don't see the problem.'

Murrin threw his head back and laughed loudly. A couple of loungers stared. 'You do stand-up?' he asked when he was done, 'Cos it's gonna be fucking impossible to stand when my boys've taken hacksaws to your feet.'

A line of sweat broke out across my forehead, but I don't like being threatened. 'Is this how you lot do business in the sticks? You've got your twenty-five grand — what more do you want? You going to steal the photos and blackmail him again?'

Murrin stubbed his fag out and stared at me. 'You really don't know, do you? I thought you had more brains.'

'Know what?'

'That little bell-end was blackmailing *me*.'

'He said his son was an actor and — '

'*My* son is filming in California. *My* money got him there and *my* money would've kept him there if it weren't for Elliott. He's too greedy. The agreement was a quarter-mil for the lot, but he only gave me fifteen photos.'

A quarter of a million pounds. I sucked on a Gauloise in an effort to appear calm. 'There are more?'

'Your man Elliott doesn't realise I had a word with the cameraman. It was difficult to hear what he was saying above the noise of the Black & Decker, but when he stopped screaming he was positive he'd taken twenty-two photos. My boys let their enthusiasm get the better of them sometimes.'

'You want me to get those photos for you.'

'Yeah, but I don't like being cheated, so I want my money back as well.'

'Sounds fair. Where and when?'

'Same place and time, tomorrow.' Murrin stood, put his fags and lighter away, and slid his big hands into his trouser pockets. 'Don't get any ideas, cos I'll be sending two car loads of boys this

183

time, and they'll be tooled.'

'I'll be there.'

★ ★ ★

At six o'clock that evening I was standing outside the Emmanuel Gallery, smoking a fag, and watching Elliott and Son. Two men left the shop at five-past, but I waited another ten minutes before repeating the previous day's performance. I'd just begun the second series of blows when a familiar figure limped into sight in the shadows of the shop. He looked surprised to see me, but he smiled and opened the door.

I stepped in, shoved him back with my left hand, gently closed the door with my right.

He staggered, swayed, and collapsed on the floor. 'For fuck's sake, I've got a prosthetic leg!'

A bit late for sympathy. I turned the keys in the lock and pocketed them. Then I grabbed Elliott by the collar of his jacket and shirt, and dragged him away from the windows, behind the till. I left him on the floor, found a shelf with gentlemen's accessories, and picked up a pack of three silk handkerchiefs.

Elliott pulled himself to his feet. 'What do you think you're doing? Wait till I tell Royston, he'll — '

I hit him in the jaw with a left, catapulting him backwards. He bounced off the wall and landed on his arse. I dropped the pack of hankies on the floor next to him, took my lock knife from pocket, and thumbed it open. As Elliott straightened up, I gripped his left wrist with my left hand, slammed it flat on the counter, and sliced off his little finger.

He screamed.

I let him have the rest of his hand back. While he threw up, I held the severed finger by the nail and sliced it in half so they couldn't sow it back on at the hospital. Then I walked over to a chair, sat, and waited. Two minutes later, he regained some kind of control of himself.

'You'll want to bind that so you don't pass out. Use the hankies.'

There was blood and vomit everywhere; Elliott was ghostly pale. He fumbled with the box, clamped the wound, and leant back against the wall, panting and sweating.

I walked over and put the knife on the till; there was too much blood on the counter. 'You thought you could get away with blackmailing a local bad boy because your cousin's a gangster?'

'Wait till I tell him what you've done. You're dead meat. Dead fucking meat.'

'Tell him what you want because I don't think he'll take too kindly to being taken for a mug. Knowing him as I do, I reckon he'll send me back for the rest of the hand. Now, to more pressing matters. I need seven photographs and two hundred and fifty thousand pounds, and I need them yesterday.' He snarled. 'Chop, chop.'

Elliott was already minus one leg below the knee and one finger at the first joint, and was obviously very attached to the rest. I bound his hand to stop him bleeding everywhere, and he took me upstairs to the safe. The briefcase was there along with five A4 manila envelopes. I opened the case and counted the money. When I was done I pointed to the envelopes. Elliott took one and placed it on top of the money. I reached for another and he started to shut the door of the safe. I bent my elbow and backhanded him across the face, sending him sprawling across the floor again.

'Honestly, Brendan, you've got to quit that. Someone's going to do you some permanent damage one day.'

I removed all four of the remaining envelopes and opened the first: a dozen photos of a fat middle-aged man having a hell of a time with an unspecified number of young women. In addition to the photos, there was a memory stick and a floppy disk. I tried the next: a very attractive natural redhead and a bloke who looked like a male model; another memory stick and another floppy disk. I put the four envelopes in a separate compartment and closed the briefcase.

Elliott was curled up in a ball.

'You'd better hope I don't come back.'

★   ★   ★

I took a taxi to the Engine Inn, arriving a good twenty minutes early. I ordered a pint of Stella, sat at a table facing the door, and stashed the briefcase underneath. I'd just swallowed my first gulp of lager when it occurred to me that I'd better double-check the magic envelope. Last night I'd had a quick glance at the contents of all of them, then destroyed the four I didn't need. What I hadn't done was make sure that all of Murrin's photos were accounted for. I cursed my stupidity, set the case on the chair next to me, and opened it a crack. There were only a couple of other punters in the pub, both of them chatting to the barman, so no one paid me much attention. I opened the envelope and pulled the photos out, making sure no one else could see.

I vaguely recognised the actor, but I couldn't be sure because it might just have been that he was a younger, slimmer version of Murrin. I looked at the woman . . .

I was nearly sick.

There was no woman, only a girl. I don't have any kids, but even I could tell she was no more than eleven. I tried the next one, more of the same. All seven of them.

I stuffed everything back into the envelope, slid it back in the briefcase, and asked the barman where the nearest post office was. Nancledra, a few minutes walk away. I bought a marker pen and sticky tape, and asked the bloke at the counter for the address of the nearest police station. Then I paid for special delivery, and returned to the pub.

Five minutes later two BMWs pulled up outside. I put the briefcase on the table, and the Taurus in my lap. Fat Man, Fat Boy, and yet another fat bastard poured out of the first car and headed for the door.

I let them come.

The Facts of the Demon Barber's Demise

Judge Turpin saw the flash of metal as the razor dipped towards his throat.

'Lucy Barker is alive!'

The blade stopped — hovered. The barber's steady hand began to tremble. 'You're a cruel bastard, ain't ya.'

Turpin felt cold, wet steel on his skin. 'Stop! You have nothing to lose and everything to gain, Mr Barker. I'm completely at your mercy.'

Sweeney Todd pulled the blade deeper into Turpin's flesh, but didn't slice. 'Go on.'

'I lied when I said Mrs Barker poisoned herself. The truth is she went half mad with grief after your . . . departure to the colonies. She's been in Bedlam ever since. Both your daughter and your wife are alive, Mr Barker, and I can reunite you.'

'What do you want in return?'

'Why, my life, of course . . . but you have to convince me I'm making the right decision.'

Todd nearly choked. 'I have to convince you your miserable life is worth saving!'

'Otherwise Mrs Barker will be forever lost to you.'

Todd considered for a moment. The razor was poised, his foot was in position on the pedal, Turpin was finally in his control. 'I'll listen, but you'd better be quick about it.'

Turpin raised a fat paw. 'Perhaps you'd be so kind? I fear your instrument is constricting my speech.'

Todd eased the pressure a fraction, but kept Turpin pressed back against the chair. He watched two crimson drops become a rivulet which sought refuge under the judge's collar.

'Thank you. Now . . . would you agree that every man in Fleet Street keeps himself clean shaven?'

'Everybody knows that,' said Todd.

'Further, that there is only one barber any man in Fleet Street would frequent?'

'Sure, ever since I sliced that prancing fairy's throat open.'

'Then there's just one more fact upon which I require your consent. If every man in Fleet Street either shaves himself or visits the famous barber, is it fair to say that the barber shaves only those men who do not shave themselves?'

Todd licked his lips. 'Yeah. When can I see my missus?'

'As soon as you've answered this question: who shaves the barber of Fleet Street?'

'The barber shaves himself, of course,' came the answer.

'Ah, but he doesn't, because we've already established that the barber shaves only those men who don't shave themselves. If he shaved himself then he would not shave himself.'

Todd let his razor hand drop to his side and his tongue protruded from his teeth. After a moment's hard thought, he replied: 'Well, he must have a beard.'

'Do any men on Fleet Street wear beards?'

'Nah, they don't.'

'And we are *speaking* of the barber of Fleet Street, are we not?'

'Yeah. I dunno, then, what's the answer?'

'Not so fast, Mr Barker. *You* must give *me* the answer in order to have Mrs Barker and Johanna restored to you, to reclaim your old life.'

Todd drew his lips back over his teeth and tapped the gleaming metal against them. He used the flat of the blade, but a tiny portion of the edge nicked his upper lip. Blood dripped down and pooled in his mouth, staining his teeth chestnut. When he smiled, he looked like he'd been chewing raw flesh. 'It's a trick, isn't it?' His left hand shot out to pin Turpin's shoulder, while his right whipped the razor back into place. 'It's Mrs Lovett and her pie shop for you, Judge.'

'It is *not* a trick, sir. There *is* an answer. If you give me that answer, all you desire shall be yours. If you fail, you will never see your wife again.'

'That's it!' Todd dropped his arm again. 'It's a woman! The barber of Fleet Street is a lady, isn't she?'

'Are you a woman, Mr Barker? We all know you are the barber of Fleet Street, so your answer doesn't solve the problem. Care to try again?'

Todd folded his arms and tapped his teeth with the razor again. A crimson thread ran down his lower lip, dripped onto his chin, and trickled down his throat.

The Judge sat still and waited patiently.

'If the barber doesn't shave himself then he must shave himself, cos that's what I agreed. But if the barber does shave himself then he will not shave himself . . . ' Todd slid the blade back and forth across his right cheek and then his left. He didn't seem to notice when he cut a long line into the latter, slicing his sideburn. The wound opened and blood poured down his face and neck, soaking into his eggplant waistcoat.

'Barker?'

'It can't be done. No, sir, it can't be done.'

'The solution is simple. A class cannot be or not be a member of itself — that is to say, there is no barber.'

'You wot?'

'The barber of Fleet Street does not exist.'

Todd brooded on the judgement for a few seconds. Then he lifted the razor and slashed his own throat open with a single, well-practiced motion.

Turpin saw the spray of blood arc over his shoulder and listened to the gurgling of the dying man behind him. Calmly, he reached for the towel and applied it to his neck. To no one in particular, he said, 'Now for Mrs Lovett. Once I've fed her the barber, I shall tell her of the baker who feeds only those women who do not feed themselves.' He cackled to himself. 'I shall enjoy watching the fat strumpet starve.'

THE END

We do hope that you have enjoyed reading this large print book.

Did you know that all of our titles are available for purchase?

We publish a wide range of high quality large print books including:
Romances, Mysteries, Classics
General Fiction
Non Fiction and Westerns

Special interest titles available in large print are:
The Little Oxford Dictionary
Music Book, Song Book
Hymn Book, Service Book

Also available from us courtesy of Oxford University Press:
Young Readers' Dictionary
(large print edition)
Young Readers' Thesaurus
(large print edition)

For further information or a free brochure, please contact us at:
Ulverscroft Large Print Books Ltd.,
The Green, Bradgate Road, Anstey,
Leicester, LE7 7FU, England.
Tel: (00 44) **0116 236 4325**
Fax: (00 44) **0116 234 0205**

Other titles in the
Linford Mystery Library:

THE MISSING HEIRESS MURDERS

John Glasby

Private eye Johnny Merak's latest client, top Mob man Enrico Manzelli, has received death-threats. A menacing man himself, he pressures Johnny to discover who was sending them — and why. Then Barbara Minton, a rich heiress, disappears, and her husband turns to Johnny. Despite Manzelli's ultimatum — that Johnny should focus on his case alone — he takes the job. But that's before he discovers the fate of the first detective Minton hired. And more bodies are stacking up . . .

NEATH PORT TALBOT LIBRARIES

A THING OF THE PAST

John Russell Fearn

Something was wrong, in and around London. Men were not shaving; women were becoming slipshod, dowdy and sullen-faced. People were bad-tempered, lacking self respect, and crime was on the increase. And, linked to these strange evidences of atavism, was a one-time excavation site. Now a mighty smoking crater, it looked as though a meteorite had descended . . . and from the vast fissure below the crater, there emerged the hideous survivors of a lost age of monster dinosaurs . . .